TANGLED LACE

KYEATE

Mz. Lady P Presents, LLC

Tangled Lace

MZ. LADY P PRESENTS

By: Kyeate

STAY CONNECTED

Facebook: Kyeate DaAuthor, Kyeate Holt & Kye Writez & Thingz
Instagram: Kye Writez
Twitter: AdjustnMyKrown

TANGLED LACE

Tangled: complicated and confused; chaotic
"A Tangled Tale"
Gates closed no more mommy and me
Hiding from my father the darkness in me.
I wanted to yell out and scream from the pain within.
Silenced by fear, keeping silent, the coward in me.
Finally helpless I had to speak
Tangled Lace he unraveled me
Piece by piece string by string
Adjusting the crown of a broken queen
Plagued of nightmares the reminders still torment
Sleep nonexistent, but the dream still exists
Life goes on to the beat of a chaotic song
My playlist, shuffle on
I am that melody, Lace Monae
I rise above the rest
Broken queen
Crown adjusted
String by string

Piece by piece
He unraveled me.

Chapter One

LACE TUCKER

2011

The water running from the faucet filled the sink, as I stood there, preparing to wash the dishes from dinner. The kitchen window in front of the sink was cracked, and the smell of weed smoke seeping through made me cringe. My father and so-called brother I used that term loosely stood outside having an after-dinner smoke. My father was in deep convo with him, and with the holes that I was burning in him, I knew he felt it because he turned to look at me. NaQuan's blinged-out grill showed as he winked at me. I quickly diverted my attention back to the dishes and finished washing them. The hatred I had for living in this house was something that I held from the outside world. Well, my best friend Brielle knew things, but it was nothing much we could do at sixteen years old.

At sixteen, I lived with my father and his new wife. My father took over custody of me when my mother went to jail in 2010 for murdering her then-boyfriend. Being ripped apart from her was devastating for my soul. It's like you go from one thing to another and then have to adjust. With my mother, we lived a different lifestyle since her boyfriend had a little money. His way of getting me to like him was spoiling me and giving me whatever I wanted. In my eyes no man could take the place of my father.

When I came to live with my father, that first year was great because it was just us, but then he met Doris Kane. Doris was sweet until she moved in. When my father proposed, and she moved in here with her son, NaQuan, shit changed. The thought of having a big brother seemed cool because he was protective and jealous-natured like any brother would be, but that all changed the moment he touched me.

The two of them came back in the house reeking of weed. I was just finishing up the dishes and was about to take it to my room and do my homework. I didn't play about school. Even though everyone would turn their nose up at me and try teasing me for whatever reason, I still managed to get my work done and maintain a 4.0 GPA.

My father had eased his way down the back hall to his and Doris' bedroom, and I headed upstairs. NaQuan sat on the couch with his phone to his ear, not taking his eyes off me as I walked upstairs.

As soon as I made it to my room, I locked the door. Sitting on my bed, I let out a huge sigh. Grabbing my back-pack, I pulled out my things and set up my stuff to do my work. Since I had done most of it before dinner, all I had to do was read over the final chapter of my history homework.

The sounds of Beyoncé's song "Love on Top" played quietly in the background. I found myself smiling hard because the song put me in a good mood. I wondered what my best friend Brielle was doing. I grabbed my phone and was writing a text when there was a knock at my bedroom door. My mood instantly changed because it could only be one person.

"Laceee!" he sang my name.

Rolling my eyes, I slowly eased off my bed and walked over to the door. Unlocking it, I cracked the door slightly. NaQuan stood there cheesing. If he weren't such an ugly soul, his smile would light up the room. NaQuan wasn't ugly, and he was quite attractive. I was no short chick, so we both stood about five foot eight inches. NaQuan was brown-skinned and had a pair of the lightest brown eyes. I didn't care to ask what happened, but he had a gash over his right eye that didn't take away from his appearance. NaQuan's body was covered in tattoos. You could tell Doris didn't care what he did because ever since they moved in, he basically does what he wants long as he went to school.

"What do you want, NaQuan? I'm doing my homework?" I asked. It was unusual for him to be upstairs this early.

"Pops asked me to bring you this. They already in bed, so let me in before I get mad!" he spat. When NaQuan got angry with me, he became a monster.

Slowly, I moved over to the side to let him in my room. Closing the door, I locked it behind me. NaQuan held his hand out, and I retrieved the folded-up money that my dad had sent up for me. The once happy place that I was at before he walked in had left, and now the uncomfortable feeling was taking over. NaQuan sat down on my bed, and I did the same, grabbing my books.

"Aye, tho, how come Brielle's ass been looking at me side-ways lately? Did you tell her something?" He spoke in a low tone. I sure did tell Brielle what he was doing. I had to tell somebody before I went insane.

"No, I didn't say anything to her, NaQuan. She probably just doesn't like you." I shrugged.

NaQuan bit down on his lip and grabbed my arm. With the grip he had, I knew it was going to leave a bruise.

"That's right because if I find out you running your

mouth, then we gone have a problem, Lace. Why you just won't let me love you?" He sighed.

I wanted to throw up in my mouth. Did he really fix his mouth to ask a question of this magnitude?

"NaQuan, this shit isn't right. You're supposed to be my stepbrother, yet you do things to me that shouldn't be done. Lines have been crossed, and that's not normal. You practically rape me and put your hands on me, not to mention you act like some jealous boyfriend," I said, jogging his memory.

"Now, I rape you? You don't be screaming that shit when I make you cum." He laughed.

He was so fucking sick. No matter how I felt each time he touched me, I didn't like that shit. Me trying to put up a fight became violent, and I just gave up. This has been going on for so long that I practically just laid there and let him have his way with me, but I couldn't stop my body from reacting to the things he would do. Did that make me a bad person?

"Nothing I do with you is consensual. It's called survival," I whispered.

The way NaQuan looked at me, I knew he was angry. NaQuan stood up and walked over to the light, turning it off. His hand pushed me back on the bed, and I said a silent prayer as he did what he did, and that was have his way with me. The way his rough hands ran over my body made me want to vomit. My expressionless face held no emotion as he rammed himself in and out of me. The sweat from his face dripped in my face, and I turned my head. When I felt him bite my chest, my eyes shot open, and he quickly placed his hand over my mouth to keep me from screaming out. *Please Lord, let him finish fast because I just wanted this to be over.*

CHAPTER TWO

As I tiptoed passed NaQuan's room, I eased out of the bath-room after handling my hygiene so that I could get ready for school. When I made it back to my room, I stood in front of my closet, looking at myself in the mirror that hung on the back of the door. Some would say I was beautiful, but I didn't think so these days. My height gave me an advantage when I used to play ball. My father was so upset when I quit playing, but it was something that I didn't have a passion for.

My skin was beautiful, minus the bruises that I had to hide. NaQuan knew to place them in places that I could easily conceal underneath my clothes. My complexion was that of ground cinnamon. I kept my hair in a weaved bob cut because I hated to deal with my real hair. It was long and curly, and that shit was for the birds. The aloe vera and witch hazel I used did my face justice, and my skin remained blem-ish-free.

Slowly, I rubbed lotion on my body and placed on my underwear. Once I finished that, I got dressed in my uniform. My phone started beeping, and I knew it was nobody but

Brielle. Not wanting to answer, I combed my hair then applied a little makeup, which was a little blush and some eye shadow to hide the stress and puffiness of my eyes. Giving myself a once-over, I was happy with my looks. Makeup wasn't a thing I always did, but it lifted my soul from the dark places. It was like I was hiding my face and pain from the people at school. Once everything was finished, I grabbed my backpack and headed downstairs.

The smell of Doris' freshly brewed coffee hit me before I made it all the way downstairs. When I hit the bottom step, she looked at me with evil eyes. To me, it was normal, but today was different. I really couldn't see why she didn't care for me, not that I cared because if you ask me, I think she knew what the hell her son was doing.

"NaQuan is waiting for you in the car, Lace," she smacked as she licked the hot coffee from around her lips.

"Aite," I mumbled and walked out the door. You see, it was hard as hell for me to escape him. He was everywhere.

When I stepped outside, I made sure to close the door behind me and used my key to lock up. Doris ass would sit at that kitchen table all day until daddy gets home from work. The sun was trying its best to peek through the cloud.

As I neared the car, the door opened from the inside. NaQuan leaned back over to the driver's side and cranked the ignition as I got in.

"Thank you," I blurted and placed my seat belt on.

The way that he could carry on as if he hasn't done anything just let me know something was wrong with him. Like after he did what he did at night to me, he goes to his room and peacefully sleeps while I cry myself to sleep. Removing my phone, I read over the texts that Brielle had sent me and texted her back letting her know that I was on the way to school.

"Who you over there texting all early? It bet not be no nigga," NaQuan said, swatting my phone out my hand, and it fell in my lap.

"Would you stop, I was texting Brielle," I groaned.

"Yeah, aite!" he spat. He reached into the ashtray and removed a blunt and lit it up as if we both weren't walking into school in about fifteen minutes.

I tuned him out and just kept my eyes out the window. I couldn't wait to get to school and get away from him. NaQuan had everyone in the damn school scared to talk to me. They thought he was being brotherly, but if they knew the real reason, things would not look good for him.

When I felt NaQuan's hand rubbing my thigh, I glanced over at him, and with his sunken eyes, he hit me with a head nod and passed the blunt my way. I wasn't new to smoking, but I sho as hell wasn't finna smoke with him.

"Lace, you be acting stuck up as hell. You need to come up out that shell." He laughed.

My insides were boiling at this fool. Something wasn't clicking right in his mind, and he needed help.

"I can't believe you really said that. Let me up out of here." I sighed and reached for the handle when we pulled into the school parking lot.

"Aye, be back here at 2:15, so I can pull out or you gone get left!" he yelled. I didn't care about him leaving me. When I stepped out of the car, I saw Brielle waiting on me being the breath of fresh air that I needed.

NaQuan Kane

I was a young nigga, but I was that nigga. People feared me, and that's just the way shit went. When my mama married Monte, I was mad as hell. I ain't gone lie. I wasn't with that blended family shit. Mama fail to realize she got little respect coming from me seeing that she ain't have me my whole life. My grandmother did up until she died when I was fifteen. Moving back with my mama, she had no clue the savage that was down in me.

When I saw Lace Monae for the first time, all that shit ceased. Them long legs, smooth looking skin, and hazel eyes had me drooling, and I ain't ever had an issue with getting a female. That brotherly shit went out the window. My thoughts for her were far from family-like. We weren't blood, so I didn't see an issue. She was my girl whether or not she liked that shit. The only reason I had to be rough with her was because she wasn't feeling that shit. If she only knew the lengths I would go for her, then life for her would be so much easier.

Shaking my head, I watched as she walked off and headed to meet her friend. I put the blunt out and sprayed some cologne on me before stepping out of the vehicle.

This was the only thing my ma asked for me, and that was to graduate. I was no dumb nigga, but I hated school. With my eyes low, I entered the building. That gas I smoked had everything heightened like a motherfucker. The slamming of lockers and millions of different conversations was ringing in my ears.

"NaQuan Kane!" I heard my name being shouted. Turning around, Principal Marshall stood there with her arms crossed and walkie-talkie in her hand.

"Yes, Ms. Marshall?" I mumbled.

"If you walk back in my school that strong again, you will be suspended for a week. Better yet, walk back up in here strong again and I will have security searching that car out there. I've been letting you off the hook because your grades are impeccable, but I'm putting my foot down. Do you understand me?" she asked with a lifted brow.

My mouth was dry as hell, and I hope she didn't think me licking my lips was at her.

"Yeah, man," I said.

"I am not a man, NaQuan!" she spat out in frustration. I could do nothing but laugh. I fucked with Ms. Marshall's old ass.

Chapter Three

LACE

Brielle and I stood in front of our lockers as she filled me in on some tea. Brielle was my heart, and we had been friends since the fifth grade. Now, Brielle was popular. Her looks and her being a cheerleader helped with her status in school. Folks would often ask why she hung with me, and she would chew them out. I wasn't the type to do what everyone else did. I was my own person, and for some odd reason, folks couldn't accept that.

Brielle looked in her locker mirror and ran her hands through her naturally curly hair. She was a little lighter than me, and her high cheekbones, deep dimples, and braces made her look so innocent. Brielle's mama was white as all get out, and her father was black, so that alone was where her complexion and hair came from.

"You stepped out with an attitude this morning, NaQuan fucking with you again?" she whispered.

Closing my locker, I turned around and leaned against the cold metal.

"When does he ever not fuck with me? You know this fool asked me last night why I won't let him love me?"

"The fuck? I can't believe I used to think he was fine as hell. Why haven't you told your dad, Lace?"

I had redirected my attention as Delmazio Davis walked down the hall. Lord, now that man did something to me. He was a senior, and he was an all-around jock. The other girls flocked to him like flies on shit. He had the longest tresses and was damn near giving every girl in school a run for their money. It was curly, and he always wore it in a knotted bun on top of his head. The few things I knew about him just from the talk around the school was that he was mixed with black and Hawaiian. The little goatee he had complimented the hairs he had above his upper lip, I don't know what they call it, but it was sexy as hell.

I assume he felt me looking because he looked my way. When he winked at me, I quickly turned my head.

"Um, anyway, I can't tell my dad, NaQuan has him wrapped around his finger. They be smoking together and everything. He is his son," I said, doing air quotes. Pushing my weight up off the locker, we started walking to class.

"I'm going to pray for you, bestie. Hopefully, this shit will end soon, but do know I will always have your back," Brielle reassured me. We hugged each other, and we headed to our classes. First period was the only one we didn't have together.

Walking into the room, I rolled my eyes at the other students.

"Lace, can I speak with you for a moment?" my teacher called out.

"Yes, ma'am?" I walked back towards her.

"I hope you didn't mind, but I have a student that has a test in my last period class. I pulled some strings, and I have you excused from your classes today so that you can go to the library and help him. I don't trust anyone else to do it, and your grades are the reason why I need this. Please say you will do it?" she asked.

From the looks of it, she had already made the decision for me.

"I guess I can," I answered hesitantly. She clapped her hands in excitement and then reached and grabbed some papers from her desk.

"This is everything you will need. I will stop through in between classes to check on you. They should already be in the library." She smiled.

Nodding my head, I grabbed the papers and headed to the library.

Stepping into the hallway, I took my time walking to the library. The papers that I held in my hand I glanced down at the name that was on paper and stopped dead smack in the middle of the hallway. Beads of sweat started to form around my edges, and my armpits started to itch.

"Nooo!" I groaned.

"Do you have somewhere you need to be?" I heard. When I turned around, it was the school's resource officer.

"Yes, I'm heading to the library," I said, showing him my papers.

"Keep it moving," he said.

Bitch! I mumbled under my breath.

Slowly, I continued the walk to the library, which now it felt like it was taking forever to get there. When I got to the door, I let out a deep sigh before entering. Soon as I walked in, I felt someone looking at me, and I turned my head, locking eyes with Delmazio. He bit his bottom lip and hit me with head nod. Flashing a nervous smile, I walked over the table.

"I'm Lace Monae. Ms. Shields sent me to help you, I guess," I said nervously. The way that he looked at me was how NaQuan looked at me before he did what he did. However, Delmazio was different.

"Well, I don't know if I want your help if you unsure about what you supposed to do," he said, cracking a smile.

I placed my books on the table across from him and pulled my chair out.

"I know what I'm here for. Let's get started," I told him.

I didn't want to have any small talk with him because he was already deep in my thoughts. I couldn't believe I was about to tutor this fine ass boy.

"Ok, so, we will start at question one at the beginning of the chapter and work our way down," I said, arranging everything.

"Do you mind moving over here? I don't want to be yelling across the table. I promise to be respectful," he teased.

The way Delmazio was flirting was how he was with the other females in school. He was a lover boy.

Not wanting to be a prude, I got up and sat in the chair next to him. I watched as he smiled and focused back on the paper that was in front of him. I took him all in the way his hairs on the side of his face curled up in the shape of a cursive S. He even smelled good. He smelled like shea butter and mangos.

Placing my hair behind my ear, I returned my focus to the task at hand and start on tutoring Delmazio. He was a great listener and a quick learner, making the session somewhat enjoyable.

———

After about another hour and a half, it was nearing lunch.

"You want to join me for lunch?" he asked. I wasn't prepared for that.

"Me?"

"Yeah, it's nobody else at the table with us." He laughed. *Why was he being nice to me?*

"I don't see why not. My stomach is growling?" I laughed.

"Trust me. I've been over here pretending that I ain't hear it, but we got to feed you, baby." I watched as he started packing up his things, so I did the same.

Walking out of the library, we headed down the hall towards the cafeteria. Trying to look as if I wasn't about to shit on myself from being nervous, I knew once we stepped in this cafeteria together, shit was most likely going to start.

When we walked through the doors, it felt like every conversation ceased. To Delmazio, nothing fazed him. He looked unbothered as we walked towards the line. My appetite seemed to vanish. I knew I looked all kinds of awkward. The smell of the slices of pepperoni pizza did make my mouth water. I grabbed a tray and followed in line behind Delmazio. Grabbing me a couple slices of pizza and a bottled water, I made my way up to the front.

"I already paid for it!" Delmazio yelled back over his shoulder.

Flashing a smile at the cafeteria lady, I headed in the same direction as him. The whispers and the stares were making me uncomfortable, and I think Delmazio could tell. We ended up at a table in the back.

Why didn't he sit with his friends?

"I hope you didn't mind sitting alone. I just wanted to talk to you without everyone being around. I've been peeping you out lately," he spoke.

"It's fine. I'm used to the gawking. What exactly have you been peeping? I blushed.

"Seeing you in the halls, and I know you probably don't believe me, but when you used to hoop, a nigga used to watch your game. Why you stop?" he asked.

"It was just something that I was doing for my father, but I never had a passion for it."

"Yeah, that's how I am about football. I play because my pops want me to live out the dream he couldn't. Basketball is my heart, though. I've already got a few schools lined up that's looking at your boy and offering scholarships."

"That's dope."

I found myself intrigued by his story and wanted to know more. I wanted to know what his hair routine was. That's how much more I wanted to know about Delmazio.

"The fuck you doing?" I jumped at the sound of the voice, and my body shut down.

Slowly, I looked up at NaQuan and could see his horns popping from his head.

"She's having lunch. What it look like?" Delmazio spoke up. *Oh no, this can't go down here.*

"Fool, I see that shit, but why the fuck is my sister having lunch with you?" NaQuan spat.

"NaQuan, I'm having lunch because Ms. Shields has me tutoring him today. We just took a break to get something to eat," I stumbled over my words, and I looked down in my lap. The way my body shut down when he came around was terrible.

"Yeah, aite, have your ass at the car on time. I'm watching yo ass," he said, pointing to Delmazio.

Delmazio chuckled and scooted his chair close to me. I had the most pleading look in my eyes, practically begging NaQuan to go away. He hit me with a slight head nod, and I knew that I would pay for this later.

"Your brother is wild," Delmazio said. I kept my head down and wouldn't look at him. I felt his warm arm wrap around me and couldn't believe this shit was happening.

"Relax girl, you good? I just watched your entire body shut down." he voiced his concern.

"I'm fine," I lied. The truth was I was scared as hell.

"Look, I know that's your brother and shit. Maybe he's looking out for you, but why you act like you scared of him?"

"He's not my real brother. My father married his mother, and he's just overprotective. That's it," I lied again. There was no way I would put all this on Delmazio.

Chapter Four

DELMAZIO "DEL" DAVIS

I wasn't blind, and I could tell the difference in how quickly Lace changed. Yeah, she was already nervous, but when her brother walked up, she froze in fear. It was the look in her eyes and the way she became tense. When I placed my arms around her, I could feel her body slowly relaxing. I didn't know what was going on, but I knew she was lying to me.

Lace was a different breed, and that's what pulled me to her. I first peeped her when she played ball, and I became fascinated with her. I had made a promise to myself that I would approach her my senior year before I left, but when she walked into the library that made my job easier. See how God works. Me being popular, I could have any girl I wanted, and trust I did. I would give all that up if I get Lace in my arms. Wanting to ease the tension, I suggested we leave the cafeteria.

"Let's leave," I blurted out as we headed back to the library. Lace's mouth crept open, and she stopped walking.

"Are you crazy? You got a test to take."

"So, if I didn't have a test, you would leave?"

"Maybe," she replied.

"Cool, I'm finna go to Ms. Shields now and take my test. You wait for me in the library, and then we can bounce if you ain't chicken."

I could tell she was already excited at the thought. She shook her head, yes, and a nigga took off down the hall.

Lace

As soon as I walked back into the library, I pulled out my phone and texted Brielle.

Me: *Bitch!!*

BB: *??*

Me: *I ended up tutoring Delmazio. We had lunch, NaQuan spazzed. I'm bout to skip school with Delmazio, cover for me.*

I knew she was going to go bonkers after sending her a summary of what happened.

BB: *Hold up, bitch. You lucky I'm in the middle of testing. You better call me soon as school let out. I need DETAILS, HOE!*

That was my girl. I placed the phone in my purse and pulled out a book I had been reading. I was currently reading *Enticed by a Cold-Hearted Menace* by Kyeate. Reading sometimes came as an escape. The things Whyte went through made me feel like maybe there was hope in this fucked-up life of mine.

I got so wrapped up in my book that I didn't notice Delmazio standing at the table.

"Must be good?" he said.

"Very," I answered.

"Come on," he whispered. I grabbed my things and grabbed his hand, and we dipped out the side doors of the library.

"Won't we get caught?" I asked in fear. My father would kill me if he knew what I was doing.

"I left out by myself and parked behind that dumpster. So,

if anybody was seen it was only me and not you. I do this all the time, though, so it's nothing. You already have your excuse from Ms. Shields, so nobody is checking for you," he said as if he had everything planned out.

When we got to his car, he hit the locks and opened the door for me. The smell of black ice and leather seem to be typical of the male species. Placing my bag in the backseat, I secured my seat belt and got comfortable.

Delmazio slid in beside me, and when he winked at me, I started feeling a little fuzzy. I watched as he pulled out the parking lot and fiddled with his phone, turning the Bluetooth on. He handed me the phone.

"Find us something to vibe to," he said.

The first name I typed in was Tyneshia Keli and played her track "I wished you loved me". Laying my head back on the headrest, I hummed along to the song and closed my eyes. I didn't know where we were going and really didn't care. Delmazio could've taken me to the moon, and I would've been satisfied. At this moment I felt free and liberated, something that I hadn't felt in a long time.

I felt bad for zoning out, so I opened my eyes and glanced over at Delmazio. He was focused on the road and moving his head to the beat.

"You like this song?" I asked.

"It's cool. It got a little message in it. Something that I can vibe to when I'm riding with my honey," he smirked.

"Well, don't be trying to play my song for any of your thots that you have in here after me," I joked but somewhat being honest.

"Hopefully, I won't have to have no other chick in here, and you'll be my girl, so you can ride shotgun all the time."

"Stop playing with me, Delmazio." I sighed. We pulled into the Exxon, and he just looked at me. The sun highlighted his light brown eyes.

"I don't know why you think I'm playing with you, girl," he said and got out the car and went into the store.

Biting my bottom lip, my mind went into overdrive. Did he really like me, or was he playing with my mind? Out of all the girls Delmazio could be with, why in the world did he want me? I was damaged goods and couldn't be good for him. What if this is a huge joke? I took a deep breath because I felt a panic attack coming. I could easily think myself into one.

Delmazio exited the store carrying a bag. He walked to the trunk before getting in the car. Instead of listening to music, we drove in silence.

"So, how old are you, Lace?"

"Sixteen, I'll be seventeen June 28th. What about you?" I answered.

"Seventeen, I turn eighteen July 16th," he replied.

We came to a stop, and I realized we were at Shelby Park. This was crazy. I used to love coming here to the duck pond.

Delmazio got out and came and opened my door. I watched as he popped the trunk and removed the bag and a blanket. Grabbing my hand, we headed towards a grassy area between the trees. I looked on in awe as he spread the blanket out and sat the bag that I now know was filled with snacks. Taking my hand, he helped me sit down, and I couldn't stop smiling.

"Nobody has ever done anything like this for me before, well being this nice period." I sighed.

"What type of people you be around? Have you ever had a boyfriend Lace?"

"I had a boyfriend in middle school. This dude name Juan Price. We dated until freshman year, and then he left the city," I shrugged.

Juan was my first love. It may have been puppy love, but I was crazy about him at one point. Sometimes I think about him because I still cared for him a little bit. When he left, things were never the same.

"That means you single and ready to mingle?"

"Why do you keep saying things like that? What do you see in me? Are you really serious right now, or is this a sick joke?" I snapped.

Delmazio squinted his eyes as if I was crazy.

"Look, I don't know why you think I would play with you about something like this. You need to let that hurt go. Yes, Lace, someone really likes you for you and nothing else. Yes, a nigga wants you to be his girlfriend because now that I finally got a chance to speak to you, I don't want to let that go. I don't care about NaQuan or nothing else. I just want you to tell me you will give me a chance to prove to you that you are everything. We can take things slow, move at your pace, but not too slow because a nigga will be graduating soon." He laughed.

Delmazio said he wanted me. He like me, and this wasn't a game.

"Ok, please be patient with me, though, because I'm a tangled mess. My life is complicated and chaotic. That's why I'm how I am," I admitted.

"Let me make those parts of your life better."

Delmazio grabbed my waist and pulled me towards him as we opened the bag of snacks and dove in while we engaged in more conversation, getting to know each other.

Chapter Five

NAQUAN

I stood outside in the parking lot waiting on Lace's mother-fucking ass. She had me fucked up. School had let out fifteen minutes ago, and she was nowhere in sight. I even went to Ms. Shields' room, and she said Lace was in the library, but when I went there, the librarian said she hadn't seen her or Delmazio. With the rage inside of me, I couldn't wait to get my hands on Lace's ass.

I hopped in the car, grabbed my blunt, and lit it up. Fuck what Marshall was talking about. Peeping the interaction after the school, I spotted Brielle in the crowd, walking towards the corner.

"Brielle!" I yelled out the window.

She looked my way and rolled her eyes. This bitch had me fucked up to. Backing out of the spot, I drove up on her ass.

"Get in, I need to talk to you," I said, rolling at a steady pace.

"I'm not about to get in the car with you!" she spat. I wasn't sure if Lace had told Brielle anything, so I had to keep my cool.

"I just wanted to know if you saw Lace. If I pull up at home without her pops gone be mad as hell." I shrugged.

Brielle stopped walking and looked at me. She was bad as hell too, but she ain't have shit on my Lace.

"I texted her towards the end of last period, and she never responded. She wasn't at the lockers either, so I left."

"Aite," I said and pulled off. I ain't know if she was lying or not, but I knew Lace was with Delmazio, and I was about to lay this on thick to pops when I got to the house.

———

Walking into the house pops was sitting in the living room, cleaning his work boots, something that he did every day and I never understood why he did that when they would get right back dirty, but I guess some folks sat in their ways.

"Waddup pops, Lace here?" I asked, knowing her ass wasn't there.

"Nah, ain't nobody walked in this house since I've been sitting here." He never took his eyes off his boots, and then the motioning of the towel slowed down as he was registering what I said. He looked up and worry etched across his aging face.

"Why ain't Lace with you?" he spat.

"I told her to wait on me when I saw her at lunch hugged up with this senior. That nigga ain't no good. He be selling weed and stuff," I threw out there.

"How you know what he sells?"

"Because I done copped from him before."

"You think Lace fucking?" Pops just flat out asked me.

The thought of that nigga getting what was mine was killing me. If it had my head gone, then I knew for a fact she would have that nigga on lock.

"Shit, I don't know what she got going on. She's all secretive and shit."

I started to twirl on the strands of my hair something that I did when I was thinking. I'm gone make that nigga not want her, or any nigga if I got anything to do with it. I chuckled at my thoughts and nodded my head. Pops had pulled out his phone, and I knew he probably was hitting Lace up.

The clicking of the lock at the front door caused me to jump up, and I walked over to the door with the quickness. Lace entered the house and I could smell him on her.

"Where the hell you been, Lace Monae?" pops yelled.

It was rare to see him pop off like that, but I guess for his precious Lace he would. I had to let her know that I wasn't messed up with her shit, so I stood there arms crossed soaking it all in.

"I had to stay after school and tutor someone for Ms. Shields. That's what I've been doing all day," she answered.

"Man, stop lying because you weren't even in the library when I came in there. She said you left with Delmazio," I jumped in.

"Lace, you out there fucking?" By this time pops was standing so close to her that I knew he was about to knock her ass out. Lace was quiet, and then she looked at me with evil eyes.

"Not Delmazio," she said.

Shit she was trying to play games.

"Don't toy with me with those smart ass replies. You being smart and you know exactly what I mean. You out here doing God knows what with who, and I swear if you bring a baby up in here your ass gone be up shit creek and homeless. Now get your ass upstairs. You got a fucking phone, and I suggest you learn how to use that shit if you got to stay after school for anything. You had everybody worried!" he yelled.

Lace stomped passed me and bumped me so hard that a nigga's skinny ass almost tipped over.

Pops took a seat on the couch, and I could tell he was stressed. Reaching deep down in my pocket, I pulled out a hundred-dollar bill and handed it to him. He looked up shocked.

"What's this?"

"I know you stressed out. You and mama go have drinks on me. Real shit, though. I don't think Lace's messing around with dude. She might have a crush though, but long as I'm around, you ain't got to worry about nothing. I got lil sis," I reassured him.

"I don't know where the hell you got his money from, but you bet not let your mama see it. I 'preciate that, NaQuan." Pops dapped me up, and he exited the living room.

Taking a seat on the couch, I grabbed the remote and changed the channel as I looked over at the steps, and the excitement that came over me was too much to control. I adjusted myself in my pants and patiently waited for ma and pops to leave.

Chapter Six

LACE

I was high and not off weed the entire drive home. Delmazio had me feeling every bit of on cloud nine. I was feeling so good that I wasn't even worried about the things that might take place once I got into the house. It was almost 4:30 and the sun was starting to set. As Delmazio pulled closer to my house, panic began to sink in, and I didn't want to alarm him.

"Pull up right here," I suggested, not wanting him to pull all the way in my driveway.

I couldn't believe that I was getting emotional because I didn't want to come down and head back to reality, and I didn't want to leave Delmazio.

"You good?" he asked. I forced a fake smile and nodded my head.

"Text me when you get settled, ok?"

"Of course," I agreed. Delmazio leaned over and placed a kiss on my cheek. My insides fluttered at the gesture.

Slowly, I eased out of the car and headed across the lawn. Dogs were barking from the nearby neighbors, and kids were outside hanging around like your average teenager would do.

Placing my key in the lock, I slowly turned the knob and

unlocked the door. Crossing the threshold, the way my father lashed out at me, I had never seen that side to him. I knew that it was nothing but NaQuan in my father's ear, especially the way he asked if I had been fucking. I wanted so bad to tell him that his favorite NaQuan was taking my innocence daily, but I just couldn't.

As soon as I got into my room, I slammed the door and tossed my backpack on the floor. Lying across the bed, I stared up the ceiling and thoughts of Delmazio, and the way our day took a turn filled my head. Who would've ever thought we would go from tutoring to acting on the crushes we had for one another? I rarely thought about sex because it was something that was forced on me, but I couldn't stop thinking about what it would be like for Delmazio to do the things that NaQuan loved doing to me.

I walked over to my bedroom window so that I could crack it open and let some of the air inside. The sound of someone laughing grabbed my attention, and I could see my father and Doris walking to the car. My body immediately tensed up, and I knew what this meant. It was like I could hear his footsteps coming up the stairs. The pounding of my heart was overpowering it.

Looking back at my bedroom door, I could see the shadow underneath that let me know he was on the other side of the door. The doorknob slowly turned.

"Lace, stop playing with me nah and open this door my girl," he slurred. NaQuan's country accent was even heavier and slower when he was high. My feet wouldn't move.

BOOM! BOOM! He banged on the door.

"You are only going to make it harder on yourself if you don't open the door!" he spat.

I slowly walked over to the door and placed my hand on the knob, unlocking it. Easing the door open, I was just ready to get this over with. NaQuan brushed passed me and stood in the middle of the floor, smelling like cologne and weed.

"You thought that shit was cool you did today, Lace? That shit hurt me seeing you with another nigga. What that nigga got that I ain't got?" he yelled.

See, this boy didn't have it all, and he showed that to me more and more each day.

"NaQuan, first of all, he isn't my brother. Second, he doesn't rape me. Those are the main things," I retorted.

"Mayne, you ain't my sister. We ain't blood, so you can kill that shit. If you think that I'm going to allow that shit, you might as well think again."

"I hate you!" I yelled.

I don't know what came over me, but the tears started to fall, and the more he talked, I just wanted to gash his eyes out. NaQuan stepped closer to me.

"I love when you talk dirty to me," he cooed.

Grabbing me by the arm, he threw me on the bed. He licked his lips as he undid his pants and stared at me as if I was the last piece of meat on the dinner plate. When he pulled his pants down, he was rock hard, and I turned my head at the sight of his penis. NaQuan roughly climbed between my legs and grabbed my face making me look at him.

"Don't make this hard for you," he whispered and planted his lips on mine.

Forcefully he slid his tongue between my lips and fiddled with my tongue since I wasn't kissing him back. I could feel him making his way to remove my pants and panties. Once he was successful, he placed his head in between my legs, and I just laid there. A tear ran down my face when I felt NaQuan's wet tongue dance across my mound. Inside my head, I was telling myself this wasn't right. I hated this part. I knew I hated NaQuan and the things he did to me.

No matter what I said in my head, my body reacted to what he was doing to me. I couldn't control the urges that came from my body. I laid there in tears and guilt consumed me as I laid there convulsing from the orgasm I just had. NaQuan stopped what he was doing, and he wiped his mouth and smiled.

"I knew you liked that shit," he moaned as he stroked himself. Turning my head, I didn't say a word as he slowly entered me. Tonight was different, and he usually would make the process a fast one, but if I didn't know any better, he was putting on a show. He was putting his feelings in what he was doing.

Chapter Seven

NAQUAN

When I first walked to Lace's room, I ain't gone lie. I had intentions of making her night hell. That shit she pulled was uncalled for. However, once I laid eyes on her, other things took over my mind. Even though I smelled his scent on her, I wasn't sure if he had touched her yet. Once I placed my face between her legs, she smelled the way that she always smelled. I knew her scent like I knew my weed. She always fronted like what we did was wrong, but her body showed me differently. When she came in my mouth, it was like something ignited inside of me, and I wanted to make love to her. I wanted to take my time. Her insides were everything and had a nigga wanting to whimper like a little bitch, but I held that shit in not letting her know that she had me so weak right now.

Everything would be so simple if she just would listen. I knew that would never happen, and I was going to do everything in my power to keep her from Delmazio's pretty boy ass. I felt my stomach tighten up, and I was about to nut. Picking up my pace, I increased my speed and placed one hand over Lace's mouth and the other around her neck.

Lace's shit was glistening around my dick, and the look of her cream brought me to another level as I shot my seeds deep inside her. Collapsing on top of Lace, my chest was still heaving, trying to catch my breath.

"Move, NaQuan!" she spat as she tried to shove me off her. I propped up a little and placed my hand back around her neck.

"I move when I get ready. You lay there and think about that shit you did today. I ain't done with you yet."

Her coughing let me know that I needed to ease up on my grip.

A nigga needed to smoke after that, but I knew I couldn't do that shit in Lace's room. Looking around on the floor, I retrieved my clothes and threw them on as I ran across the hall to my room. A nigga kept a blunt rolled, and I grabbed one off my dresser and took that shit to the head. Thoughts of how Lace's body reacted to mine while I was inside of her, I knew she was enjoying that shit, and she couldn't tell me differently. I knew once I finished this blunt that I was going to be ready for another round, and I was gone get my shit before moms, and Monte made it back to the house.

After finishing off the blunt, I walked back across the hall. Lace was balled up in a fetal position in the bed. I lifted the cover and scooted behind her. She was tense as hell and jumped at my touch. Blowing out in frustration, I didn't even feel like fucking fighting with her. I used my hand to slightly lift her leg enough for me to slide in. The entire time I was hitting her with thrusts, she was crying. That shit was pissing me off. After a couple more strokes, I shot off in her. Snatching my dick out, I tossed the blanket and left her lying there.

Lace

I wanted NaQuan to die a slow motherfucking death. He didn't care about shit, so it was no point in me even playing sleep. I was so glad when he carried his ass up out of here. There was no way I was getting up to shower right now, at least while daddy was gone. My legs trembled as I tried to stand and retrieve my phone off the dresser. Once I grabbed it, I climbed back in bed and placed the covers over my head. I scrolled to Delmazio's number and stared blankly at it. Did I want to text him? I was tired of feeling the pain that I felt. Delmazio made me feel like there were no problems.

The slamming of the car door caused me to jump, and I sat quietly. I even stopped breathing for a few seconds. Once I heard the alarm beep, I knew they had made it back home. Sliding the phone underneath my pillow, I grabbed my robe and my pajamas rushing to the bathroom.

The scalding hot water was enough to kill the germs that were embedded in my skin and the DNA of a sick ass individual that I wanted off my body. I scrubbed my skin until it was red and raw. No way would I let a tear drop or sound come out my mouth to where NaQuan could hear me.

I stepped out of the shower and dried off, placing my pajamas on. Standing at the door, I eased it open slowly so that it wouldn't make a sound. The coast was clear, so I ran back across the hall to my room and locked the door.

I climbed in bed and retrieved my phone from underneath my pillow. Scrolling to Delmazio name, I sent him a text.

Me: *U up?*

I laid the phone on my chest and waited on a response back. It was a little after midnight. Closing my eyes, the vibration that hit my chest excited me. Picking up the phone it was Delmazio texting me back.

Del: *U straight? I was just thinkin' bout you real shit.*

Me: *You've been on my mind since you left. I hate it here.*

Del: *You straight? Everything good?*
Me: *Nothing's ever good here.*
Del: *Maybe we can link this weekend.*
Me: *I would love that. GN Del.*
Del: *Hit u in the a.m. GN beautiful.*

After talking with Delmazio, he put my mind at ease enough to be able to go to sleep. I wanted sweet dreams with nothing but the two of us in it.

———

The sun beaming on my face woke me up out of the deep slumber that I was in. I slowly blinked, letting my eyes adjust. Glancing at the clock, I saw that it was 10:34 a.m. on a Saturday. I wanted nothing more but to get dressed and head to Brielle's house. I couldn't move, though. My energy was scarce. I didn't feel my best. My body ached, and I felt soulless as if the ounce of soul I had left detached itself from my body. The faster I got up, the quicker I could get up out this house and get to Brielle's. After having that thought, I kicked the cover off me and hopped up. I grabbed a pair of sweat pants, and a t-shirt then headed to the bathroom to wash my face and brush my teeth.

When I entered the kitchen to fix me some breakfast, my father was sitting at the table. I felt his eyes following me. I felt nasty as if he could see everything.

"Lace, sit down," he demanded.

I turned towards him, walked to the table, and took a seat. He placed the paper down and pinched the bridge of his nose.

"Lace, I know you are going through that stage where you're getting older and secretive. As your father, I want you to tell me the truth about yesterday," he voiced.

"I told you the truth. I tutored a student, and that was it.

I don't know what NaQuan put in your head, but it isn't the truth. He just doesn't like Delmazio for his own selfish reasons!" I spat, saying a little too much.

"His own reasons like what? Why would he have issues with that boy?"

"Nothing, girl issues, I guess. Look, I'm sorry I didn't call and let you know. I didn't think I did anything wrong. NaQuan be walking around trying to be somebody daddy, and it's embarrassing. He be showing his ass at school." I sighed.

"Watch your mouth. He is doing what any brother would do for their sister. Are you having sex?" he blurted out.

I paused for a moment, not sure how to answer his question. I wanted to be truthful, but I knew I couldn't be all the way truthful.

"I have had sex, but not with who I was with yesterday." I could tell by the look in his eyes that I hurt him with my response.

"I still see you as my little girl. You will always be my little girl, no matter how old you get. Just protect yourself because I don't want you to throw your life away for some knuckle-head ass little boy." My father sighed. I smiled, hearing him call me his little girl done something to me.

"Can I go over Brielle's for the weekend?" I asked since things seemed to be on the up and up. My father shook his head.

"Nope, you still on punishment, but she can come over here and stay if she wants," he scooted his chair out and got up from the table. Leaning forward, he placed a kiss on my forehead and walked out of the kitchen.

Chapter Eight

BRIELLE SIMMONS

The sounds of laughter filled the room while Lace and I sat on the floor listening to music and having girl talk. The smiled that graced her face I enjoyed seeing.

"I'm dead ass, Lace, when you said you were leaving with Delmazio, girl I wanted to the run-up out the classroom!" I shouted.

"It's still like unreal to me. He makes me feel so liberated." Lace sighed and looked down at the floor.

There it was. She was shutting down. I had known Lace long enough to pick up on the signs when things happened to her.

"Talk to me, Lace. I know something happened," I voiced while I rubbed her shoulder.

"Last night after my dad and Doris left, of course, NaQuan made his way in here, and he raped me. This time it just felt different. He was really upset about the Del thing."

"I think you need to go to the police. If you won't tell your dad, you need to tell someone before things get out of hand, Lace," I voiced.

"My dad asked me this morning was I having sex. I

wonder would he believe me if he knew the things that were going on under his roof."

"Lace, I hate to tell you this, but the longer you hide this, it will not end well. This shit is going to come out whether you want it to or not. I just got a feeling," I admitted. Everything that's done in the dark eventually comes to light.

"Brielle, you can't say anything!" Lace's voice shrieked in terror.

"Who said I was going to say anything? I'm talking in general."

Lace

I didn't mean to snap on Brielle, but I took what she said all wrong. Me confiding in her was because I felt comfortable, and I just prayed that she kept her word and was just speaking in general.

Brielle and I laid around watching movies and staying locked in my room all the while Delmazio and I FaceTimed most of the day. I hated that I couldn't leave out so that I could see him, but it was the next best thing.

I glanced at the time on the clock, and the house was now silent. Pops and Doris had recovered to their room for the night. Sitting in the window seal, I stared out watching for the signal I was looking for. I knew I wasn't supposed to leave the house, but I would do anything just to physically have Delmazio in my presence. I needed to feel his energy and feed off it. Delmazio said he would park alongside the street and flash his lights. We agreed to meet at the vacant house that was on the corner.

"You nervous?" Brielle asked. Glancing at her, I flashed her a smile and shook my head.

"No, and at this point, I don't even care if I get caught." I sighed, looking back out the window. The flashing of lights in the distance made me perk up.

"He's here. You sure you're going to be ok?" I asked.

"Yes, I'll be fine. Go see your man." Brielle smiled.

I grabbed my hoodie, pulling it over my head. Placing my ear against the door, I made sure no one was in the hall. Cracking the door, the coast was clear, and NaQuan's door was closed. Slowly I eased out the room and made my way downstairs. My heart was beating so fast that I could hear it. Once I got out the front door, I reached down under the broken brick and removed the key I placed there earlier. The way I ran down the sidewalk you would've thought somebody was chasing me. Delmazio stood off in the dark dressed in black. As I approached him, his smile soothed me. Jumping in his arms, I squeezed him so hard.

"Dang, you miss a nigga like that?" he laughed. Looking at him, he had no idea.

"You have no idea. This punishment shit is beyond me," I sighed.

We held hands and walked in the backyard of the vacant house. The moonlight lit the backyard just enough for us to see each other. Taking a seat on the back steps, he pulled me close and wrapped his arms around me. Just being in his arms done something to me. It ignited a fire inside. I wanted him in the worse way, and I didn't know why. I leaned in and planted a kiss on his lips. Pulling away, he looked at me with confusion. Grabbing ahold of his face, I climbed in his lap and kissed him with so much passion. Reaching for his shirt, I let my hands roam his washboard abs and wanted him out of the shirt.

"Hold up, girl," he panted. At that moment, I felt embarrassed that I couldn't control whatever it was that was going on with me.

"I'm sorry," I mumbled.

"Listen, I want this as much as you do, but for some reason, I think you want it for other reasons. Maybe you're vulnerable right now, and you're not thinking straight. This ain't the right time, Lace," Delmazio said with so much compassion.

My shoulders slumped in defeat because he read me like a book.

"If you were somebody else, I would give you the business, but Lace, you're my girl, and I respect you," he whispered and rubbed the side of my face.

Slowly I climbed out of his lap and took my seat beside him. Placing my head on his shoulders, I was speechless.

Brielle

I laid here watching *All American* on Netflix trying to stay up because Lace had been gone for quite some time. The jiggling of the doorknob caught my attention, and I quickly glanced at the door. Easing up, I slowly tiptoed over there.

"Lace!" he whispered. It was NaQuan's nasty ass.

The doorknob turned again, and this time I jerked the door open and looked him dead in the eyes, which were low as hell. His ass stayed high.

"What do you want?" I sassed, blocking the doorway so that he couldn't see in the room. I prayed that she didn't come back while he was here.

"Man, tell Lace to come here."

"No can do. You got to keep your dick in your pants tonight, nasty ass!" I spat. Licking his lips, I wasn't sure how he would respond.

"The fuck you talking about?"

"Just know I know what you be doing to my best friend, and I promise you will pay for that shit. I advise you to go back to your room," I spoke with so much confidence. Inside I was scared as hell, but I couldn't show him I feared him.

I watched as he backed away and headed down the steps. I stood there and heard the front door open and close. Rushing to the window, I watched NaQuan hop in his car and pull off. Looking at the clock, I saw it was after midnight. Grabbing my phone, I sent Lace a text just to make sure she was ok.

Me: *Lace, NaQuan just left out of here pissed. Get home!*

I laid back on the bed and placed my phone on the nightstand.

———

"Brielle!" slowly opening my eyes, I realized I had dozed off, and Lace was waking me.

"What time is it?" I groaned.

"It's 2:30 a.m. What the hell happened?" she asked. I sat up on the bed.

"Is NaQuan back?"

"His car was out front. What's going on?"

"I was sitting here watching TV, and he tried to get in the room. He was playing with the doorknob and shit, so I opened the door, asking what he wanted. He asked for you, and I told him he wasn't sticking his dick in you tonight. I also let him know that I knew what he was doing and one day he would get his." I shrugged.

"The fuck, Brielle?" she whined. Lace was scared shitless.

"You lucky he ain't try no shit with you. I couldn't have that shit on my conscious. I know he gone flip out when he sees me." She sighed.

We both sat there in silence consumed in our thoughts.

Chapter Nine

NAQUAN

That bullshit Brielle's light bright ass let fly out her mouth last night had me wanting to go in her shit, but I had to keep my cool. I left because if I had stayed another minute, I would've done some foul shit. So, this entire time, I kind of had a feeling that Lace had told Brielle what was going on, but what the fuck was that threat about she let come out her mouth? I made sure not to cross paths with both they asses today. With it being Sunday, I knew Monte wouldn't let Brielle stay late. As soon as she left, I was going to have a little talk with Lace.

Mama was in the kitchen, putting her foot in Sunday dinner. After cleaning my room, I grabbed my blunt and headed to the backyard. Monte was back there washing ma's car. I sat down and lit the blunt. As soon as he got a whiff of this loud, I knew he would stop what he was doing. Taking a long drag, I blew the smoke out and zoned out.

"Where you head off to last night?" Monte called out.

"What you talking about?" I asked, trying to play stupid. Monte walked up to me, removed the blunt out of my hand, and took a hit.

"You left the house twice last night," he said, passing me back the blunt. I was about to answer but decided not to just yet.

I pulled my phone out, pulled up the alarm app, and watched the cameras from last night. Making sure to watch at the time I left, I kept watching until I saw Lace ass walking up on the porch. *When the hell did she leave?*

"Yeah, I had a lot of shit on my mind last night, so a nigga had to dip," I lied.

I kept watching the cameras going back to earlier in the evening before I left and sho nuff Lace had left the house. My jaws grew tight because I bet her ass snuck out to see that nigga. I'm gone knock her ass out.

The venom that shot through my body had a nigga trembling. That shit had me so antsy that I couldn't hold still. Monte handed me back the blunt, and I hit that shit hard as hell.

"You out here having girl problems?" He chuckled. One thing about Monte I didn't have to hide who I was because he kept it G. It wasn't like he was my real dad anyway.

"More like hoe problems. These females don't know shit about loyalty and who's really down for them and shit," I said, throwing all kinds of shade at his daughter.

"Well, that's that young generation for ya youngin'. You ain't gone find too many females like your sister." He chuckled.

I looked at this man like he was crazy. My nigga, I hit the blunt so hard I started choking.

"I'm done with these hoes," I said, standing up. Dusting off my jeans, I handed him the remaining of the blunt and went inside. When I entered the house, ma was finishing up dinner.

"Tell them to come on down here and get ready to eat,"

she called out as I walked past the entryway. I nodded my head and headed upstairs.

As soon as I hit the top step, Lace and Brielle were coming out the room. Whatever was being said had come to a halt, and we all locked eyes. Lace wore a look of nervousness, and Brielle wore a snide smirk on her face.

"My mama said for y'all to go eat," was all I said and walked towards Lace. She tried to move furthest to the wall, but the look I gave her let her know that I wasn't about to play with that ass later. Grabbing my dick, I hit her with a wink and headed to my room.

———

Sitting at the table, a nigga was high as hell and mama had indeed put her foot in this food. Everybody was wrapped up in different conversations. The only thing on my mind was choking the hell out of Lace.

"Lace, do we have an understanding now since you had plenty time to think this weekend about your actions?" Monte asked her.

Lace rolled her eyes and then looked at me.

"I guess." She shrugged.

"You guess? You need to stop running around here with these little boys that mean you know good. I ain't raising no babies!" my mama snapped.

I don't know where that shit came from.

"I ain't running around with nobody. It's more like running away from something." Lace smirked.

"I know that's right," Brielle mumbled. These hoes wanted to play.

"You got something to say?" I blurted out.

"Yeah, I do. You wrong for lying on me. You know the truth!" Lace had the nerve to say.

"Man, this shit ain't got nothing to do with me. Like they said, you need to stop running around with Del. That nigga ain't shit. Since you want to be smart, I ain't taking the wrap for your ass. That wasn't me last night leaving, Monte. That was your precious daughter sneaking out." I laughed.

Lace wanted to play. Let's go, hoe. Her mouth flew open, and Monte looked at her with evil in his eyes.

"Is NaQuan telling the truth, Lace?" Monte spat. I pulled my phone out and pulled up the app in case I had to show him the video.

"Yes," was all she said with tears in her eyes.

One thing I knew about Lace, no matter what I did to her, she wasn't about to speak on that shit because she knew she was going to have to pay for that shit.

"Brielle, you need to call your ride because it will be a minute before Lace has company again," Monte said and stood up from the table, shaking his head.

"Lace, don't you think about leaving this house for shit!" Monte yelled over his shoulder.

Chapter Ten

LACE

To say I couldn't believe NaQuan would be a lie because that was just how dirty he was. The way he threw me under the bus was downright dirty. I had completely lost my appetite and removed myself from the table. Brielle followed closely behind me, calling her ride to come pick her up. Walking into my room, I plopped down on the bed and let out a huge sigh. Brielle started gathering her things since her ride was on the way. My mind drifted to Delmazio, and I needed to send him a text just in case my dad came up here taking my phone. The way he walked off, I knew he was mad, and he had to think of what he was going to do to me.

Reaching for my phone, I scrolled to Delmazio's number.

Me: *Hey, NaQuan snitched on me about last night, so if you don't hear from me, I don't have my phone.*

I was expecting a text back, but instead my phone started ringing. Quickly I answered the phone.

"Why is that nigga always hating?" Del spat.

"He just be on some fuck shit. My dad was mad as hell and left the dinner table, so I don't know if he is going to do anything else. I know I can't leave the house." I sighed.

"Don't even worry about all that. We will see each other at school, and you know that I will make a way. I see now I'm gone have to say something to your brother, though."

"No!" I quickly shouted.

"Lace, why do I feel like you're keeping something from me, shorty? I can tell by the way your body reacted when he came up to the lunch table. Do that nigga be fighting on you or something?" he asked.

I could hear footsteps nearing my door.

"I have to call you back someone's coming," I whispered and hung up the phone. Sliding the phone underneath my pillow, Brielle and I both had our eyes locked on the door. There was a light knock and then my door opened. Once I saw that it was my dad, I was somewhat relieved but irritated because I didn't want to hear his mouth.

"Brielle, you can go downstairs and wait on your ride, I need to have a talk with Lace," he said, looking at Brielle.

Brielle looked at me, and I gave her a nod letting her know that I would talk to her later. Once she left the room, my father let out a deep sigh, and the wrinkles in his forehead let me know that he was stressed.

"Lace, what is going on with you child?" He sighed. Shaking my head, I looked at him.

"Nothing is going on with me, you just seem to believe NaQuan's word over mine, and I'm your own flesh and blood. I told you the truth the other day when you asked me. I'm not out here having sex with boys. Yes, I did sneak out yesterday, but nothing happened. The person that I'm dating is respectful and nothing like that. NaQuan lies a lot, and one day you're going to stop putting your trust in him," I mumbled, holding my head down.

I wanted so badly to tell my father the things that were happening to me underneath his own roof, but it just wouldn't come out.

"I don't know what you expect me to think because you've been so secretive lately. We have never had any issues now. If I didn't know any better, I would say you are wanting some attention. Have you talked to your mama?" he asked.

I couldn't believe he fixed his mouth to say that I was acting out for attention. This was the shit I was talking about. He couldn't see shit wrong with NaQuan, and it was putting a strain on our relationship. His head was so far up Doris' ass that he couldn't think for himself.

"You know what. I'll just take whatever punishment you are about to give me because I'm done talking, and I just want to lay down," I stood up and started gathering my things for a shower. The disappointed look on my father's face let me know that I had let him down once again.

"Lace, what do you plan on doing with your life? Do you want to end up out here on the streets? You gave up basketball, but yet you don't do anything else to occupy your time."

"I gave up basketball because that was your passion, not mine. I hate basketball. I did that to make you happy. I just lost my mother to the system, and honestly, I have a lot on my plate right now. I make the best grades in school. I get picked on, and I stay to myself. You act as if I'm out here running the streets stirring up trouble. Sadly, the only thing you see coming from me is a fuck-up, like you claiming shit I want no parts of. Are you done?" I asked.

"You just make sure you bring your tail home after school until further notice!" he spat before walking out.

As soon as he left, I headed to the bathroom and took care of my hygiene.

Once I was done, I eased back across the hall to my room and closed the door. Locking the door, I eased on to the bed and climbed underneath my covers. It was still daylight outside, but my body needed rest, and I just wanted to sulk in my thoughts.

Chapter Eleven

DELMAZIO

Over the last two weeks, Lace and I had to sneak around seeing each other. Whether it was at school or small periods after, we couldn't get enough of each other. Beads of sweat rolled down my forehead as Lace laid her head on my shoulder, catching her breath. It was lunch, and we had snuck off campus and had a quickie. The chemistry between the both of us had increased over the past two weeks.

"Dammit, girl, where is this sexual appetite come from?" I asked with labored breaths.

Lace climbed out of my lap and started grabbing for her shirt. This was our second time having sex. At first, I wasn't trying to go that route with her just yet, but she was adamant, so I gave in. Looking over at Lace, I noticed a few dark spots on her back that looked like bruises.

"Lace, what the fuck happened to your back?" I asked.

Lace quickly pulled her shirt down and held her head down in shame. I finished getting dressed, but we were about to get to the bottom of this.

"Did your dad put his hands on you?" I spat.

Lace shook her head no. I didn't know what to think, but

I was mad as hell. Running my hands over my face, I let out a frustrated sigh.

"Lace, what the fuck's going on with you? Whatever it is, it's time to come clean, no more hiding shit. Can't nobody help you if you're keeping secrets?"

"There are some things I need to tell you, but I'm scared you may judge me," she cried. Reaching over, I grabbed her hand, placed it in mine, and used my other hand to lift her head.

"I promise I won't judge you. You just have to make me understand if it's that bad," I told her.

Lace wiped her tears.

"When my father married NaQuan's mom, I was excited to have a big brother because he was protective of me and stuff. Things changed, and I realized his protective ways was him being jealous because he wanted me to himself. At night, NaQuan makes his way into my room and rapes me. He doesn't think it's rape or sees anything wrong because we're not related by blood. He put his hands on me as well when I do things he doesn't like or try to fight him. He's been feeding my dad all this bad stuff about you in hopes that I will stay away from you. NaQuan is fucking crazy," Lace cried.

My mind was racing and I was letting what she said replay in my mind. Did she just say what I think she said?

"How long has this shit been going on? Why you ain't told your pops or called the police on his ass? That's some sick shit!" I yelled.

"A long time. NaQuan has my dad wrapped around his finger. He doesn't think NaQuan can do any wrong. To make matters worse..."

Lace placed her hands on her face and cried so hard you would've thought I was hurting her in the car. This shit was freaking me out.

"Lace, what is it man? You scaring a nigga," I pried.

"I just found out I was pregnant, and there is no way in hell, I'm having this fucking baby," she snorted through tears.

Nigga, that shit through me all off. I leaned so far away from her because all this shit thrown at a nigga at once was not expected. Then my mind drifted.

"Were you having sex with me all this time so that you could try to plant this baby on me?" I asked.

You would've thought a nigga had two heads the way that Lace looked at me. Lace started to put on the rest of her clothes in silence.

"Take me back to the school now. I can't believe you even let some shit like that come out your mouth," she hissed.

I had nothing to say because hell what else was I supposed to think. Once we got situated, I drove us back to school. Thinking about what she just shared with me, I felt compelled to protect her, but still, in the back of my mind, I wondered why all of a sudden she had the urge to have sex.

Pulling into the parking lot, I turned the car off, and Lace went to open the door. Reaching out, I grabbed her arm.

"Hold up. I know I said some fucked up shit, but you can't drop all the shit you dropped on me then expect me to walk around like you ain't just told me shit. If you look at the situation, you can't knock me for asking that. You supposed to be my gal, so we gone have to find a way to keep that nigga out your room if you're not going to tell nobody," I suggested.

"I need to get rid of this baby, Del. I don't want no parts of his ass inside of me. That's the first thing I need to take care of."

"I know you want to get rid of the baby, but that could be your proof as well to your family what's going on. They need to know."

"You don't know his mama. She will swear up and down that I've been fucking him on my own and not him raping me. Del, I need your help." she sighed.

Biting down on my bottom lip, I thought about helping her, and I didn't mind. I had a suggestion, but she might not be satisfied with it.

"Look, I'm gone have to tell my ma that I got you pregnant, and we need to get you an abortion. My aunt works at Planned Parenthood, so she can maybe pull some strings since you sixteen if my ma talks to her. Just stick it out for a few days and start recording that nigga if you got to set your phone up or some shit to catch his ass in the act," I told her.

Using my hand, I pulled Lace towards me and placed a kiss on her forehead.

"Go on to class. We gone get through this," I told her.

Lace got out of the car, and I watched as she made her way in the building. Laying my head back on the seat, I knew once I told my ma this shit, she was going to hit the fan. The one thing she told my ass was not to fuck these girls out here unprotected. One thing I knew for a fact though was keeping my cool around NaQuan because the way I'm feeling I'm liable to fuck him up. A nigga prayed like hell we could get this shit handled because I don't think I could stick with her if she had NaQuan's baby.

Chapter Twelve

LACE

The last two weeks of my life had been a living hell. On top of being on punishment, that meant that I had to spend a lot of time in the house and with NaQuan. My father made sure that he took me everywhere I needed to go. I had to check-in and do all that. When I came to school, I would sneak off with Del and suck up all the time that we could get together.

Things took a turn when I found out I was pregnant. Nobody knew what was going on, not even Brielle. I was devastated, and honestly, Del called me on my shit, but I had to act as if what he was saying wasn't true. I planned to lie to him after a while and tell him I was pregnant by him because I had no way to get the abortion. I had thought about telling NaQuan, but his dumb ass would've sworn up and down it was Del because he had it out for him.

I was going to let Del do what he could and prayed like hell that it worked, and we could get this taken care of immediately because there was no way I was going to walk around carrying the spawn of Satan. When I made it to my locker, Brielle was standing there with attitude all over her face.

"I'm glad you made it back in time because I can't keep

covering for you. You and Del need to find other times to fuck." Brielle laughed.

"Shut up. Did you see NaQuan?" I asked, removing my book for the next class out of my locker.

"Nope, but there his ass go right there." Brielle rolled her eyes and pretended to be busy in her locker.

I could feel NaQuan's presence behind me. I didn't even bother to turn around. The knots in my stomach started to form, and I could feel the vomit building up in my mouth. Placing my hand on the locker, I took deep breaths to try to remove the feeling that just came over me.

"You good?" Brielle asked.

"The fuck wrong with you?" NaQuan spat. Slamming my locker, I turned to face him.

"Nothing, did you need something?" I asked.

"Why you weren't at lunch?"

"Because I didn't feel good, and I was lying down in the nurse's office. Anything else? I need to get to class."

"You know the deal. Have your ass at the car after this class. Ain't nobody finna be waiting around for you all day," he said, referring to when it was time to go home.

NaQuan walked off, and Brielle and I headed in the other direction to class.

———

The time had come for us to leave school, and I just wanted to lie down. During the ride home, I was in and out of it with my thoughts.

"What's been your problem?" NaQuan looked over at me and asked. All I did was shake my head.

"You think a nigga don't know when something wrong with you. I know you better than you know yourself." He chuckled. That was the thing I hated the most. He was connected to my innermost parts.

"I'm fine, NaQuan, please just leave me alone." I sighed.

"You must be finna come on. I noticed you ain't came on your cycle yet," this nigga said.

Shaking my head, I prayed like hell he stopped with the questions and shit.

"I'm cramping now," I lied. *Jesus, if he don't hurry and get my ass home.*

The look on NaQuan's face softened, but that shit meant nothing. That's just the way he was. The bruises etched across my back were because we hadn't been on the best of terms since he found out about me sneaking out the house. I figured that night after dinner he was going to let me have it, but he waited until I least expected it. The sex was rougher, and honestly, if I didn't know any better, I think he was trying to get me pregnant on purpose.

We pulled up into the driveway, and he didn't cut the car off. I grabbed my bag and started to get out of the car.

"I'll be back in about an hour. I got to make a quick run," he said.

Slamming the door, I made my way into the house. The house was quiet which was weird because Doris' ass usually be in the kitchen at the table, but she wasn't there.

Once I saw nobody was at the house, I rushed up the steps two at a time and threw my bag in my room. Walking back to NaQuan's door, I slowly turned the knob and eased the door open. Shockingly his room was spotless and organized. It was the perfect set up for a psycho anyway.

Standing there, my mind drifted to where might he keep his money stashed. I knew what I was about to do was risky, but it was a chance I was willing to take. Moving around NaQuan's room slowly and being careful not to move anything out of place, I looked in his drawers and underneath his bed. After coming up short in both of those areas, I made my way to his closet. NaQuan was a fucking shoe freak, and the way he had his shit organized was neat as hell, even his clothes were color-coordinated.

Looking at the many shoeboxes, one stood out. The raggedy edges and discoloration made it shine bright. Grabbing the box, I remember which box was sitting on top of it, and I opened the box. God had to be on my side because this shit was filled with money. All the money was rolled up into knots, so I carefully removed a hundred-dollar bill from the center of six rolled knots and placed the box back where it was.

Coming out of the closet, I closed the door back and made my way back to my room. Grabbing my phone, I sent Delmazio at text.

Me: *I got the money for that, so let me know something soon.*

Chapter Thirteen

NAQUAN

Lace thought a nigga was stupid, but as I told her, I knew her better than she knew herself. She was already standoffish with me most of the time, but she was hiding something. That pussy was even hitting different, which lead me to believe that she was fucking that nigga Delmazio too. The words I was waiting for though was for her to tell a nigga she was pregnant. A part of me was happy, but then the other half wasn't sure if I was the daddy or Delmazio.

Lace and I weren't blood related, so I'm sure if we told our parents the truth and that we loved each other that they would be ok with the baby. Shit could work out if she just gave the fuck in and stop playing all the time. I wasn't a bad person. The entire time I was out making runs, I couldn't keep Lace off my mind.

———

A few hours later, I was high as hell, making my way in the house. Monte and my mom were cuddled up on the couch watching TV. I nodded and headed straight to the kitchen to fix me something to eat.

When I entered the kitchen, Lace was on the phone, and she was washing dishes. She didn't even know that I was in there. Taking her in from behind, the way she stood there, and her ass sat up right in the leggings she had on had a nigga wanting to take her right here and now. I guess she felt somebody watching her, so she turned around, and we locked eyes. She quickly turned around and finished what she was doing. All I did was laugh and proceeded to fix me something. I threw the knife and utensils I used in the sink.

"I'm not washing that out," Lace mumbled.

"Stop being a bitch. Just wash it out. You're already washing dishes!" I yelled.

"No, you wash your own shit out. You didn't even have to use that shit. You only did it because you saw me washing shit up!" Lace spat, throwing the rag on the counter and exiting the kitchen.

I swear she was trying my ass, and I wasn't about to let her blow my high. A nigga grabbed my shit and headed upstairs.

"What's wrong with Lace?" Monte asked.

"I don't know. She got an attitude like always," was all I said.

I kept walking, and when I got upstairs, Lace had slammed her door. I shook my head and went to my room. Sitting the plate on my dresser, I reached into my jeans and removed the money I had and grabbed some rubber bands. After counting and wrapping, it up I went to my closet and removed the box I kept my money in. Removing the money, I laid them flat across the dresser and lined them up. Some of my rolls were off, and I could tell by the roundness of the wrap. I grabbed one of the knots and counted it. I had a thousand dollars in each wrap, and this particular one counted up to nine hundred. I continued to count the other wraps, and I was missing six hundred dollars.

My mind drifted off because maybe my ass was higher than I thought. I counted my money twice and kept coming up with the same shit, so the next thing was who in they right mind was stupid enough to come in my shit and take my money. My mama didn't rock like that. She knew she could ask me for anything. Hell, she doesn't even come in my room without knocking. Monte doesn't even do that shit.

Storming out my room, I went across the hall to Lace's room. I didn't want to just go off because I could be wrong, so maybe I could try a different approach. I tapped on the door lightly.

"What?" Lace called out.

"I need to talk to you for a minute," I mumbled.

I could hear movement behind the door. The door flew open, and Lace looked at me like I was crazy. I don't know where this new set of balls came from, but she wasn't the timid Lace that I had shook if I even yelled at her. Shoving her into her room, I locked the door behind me and walked up on her.

"Suddenly, you big and bad and shit, walking around with this new attitude, you got something you need to tell me?" I questioned her seeing if I could read her because somebody in this house took my damn money.

"Matter of fact, I do have something I need to tell you," she smirked.

"What's that? You took six hundred dollars out of my closet?"

"I ain't even been in your room, so don't put that shit on me. What I do know is that you need to come up on some money because I'm pregnant."

"What you telling me for, ain't you fucking that Del nigga?" I spat.

"No, I'm not. I'm telling you because now your dirty ass secret is about to come out when Doris and my daddy find out I'm pregnant." She shrugged.

"If they fucking find out, you ain't killing my seed. We need to go to them together and tell them how we feel about each other so that we can raise our kid."

"Do you fucking hear yourself, NaQuan? Nigga, this baby ain't made from no love. This shit is a product of rape. I hate you, and I ain't ever gone be what you want me to be!" she cried.

Walking up on her, I placed my hands tightly around Lace's neck.

"I know you went in my room and took my money!" I spat.

"I haven't stepped foot in your room," she panted, clawing at my arms.

Releasing her, I shoved her on the bed and gave her a deathly stare. Walking back out the room, I left out like a thief in the night.

The last week had been stressful as hell. That day when NaQuan came into my room accusing me of stealing his money, I just knew he was going to hurt me. There was no way I was going to admit to taking it. Yeah, it was dumb of me to tell him that I was pregnant, but that was the only way I could get him to confess what he was doing to me. The entire conversation I was recording on my phone, and he didn't even know. That was my ticket, and I had enough to convince anyone I told. I can say that NaQuan had kept his distance this week, and that was strange.

Del came through on his part, and his mother pulled some strings to get me into the clinic, no questions asked. The money I stole from NaQuan paid for the abortion pill that was given to me. The process was scary because I had to do a lot of ass-kissing to get my dad to let me stay with Brielle this four-day weekend. It was the day after, and I felt like shit.

Yesterday Del's ma took me to the clinic, and she was the sweetest lady. I thought she was going to be stuck up and mad thinking that I was trying to ruin her son's life because he did tell her I was carrying his baby, but she was far from that. Due to Del's aunt being there, we avoided the usual process far and them trying to talk me out of the decision and all of that. This baby had to go, and I refuse to bring the spawn of NaQuan in this world. I was nervous because I didn't know what to expect, but I took a pill at the clinic, and she told me soon as I got home to take the other one.

Delmazio's mama let Brielle and I stay over at her house so that she could watch me. When we got to her house, I was scared as hell to take the other pill. As soon as it touched my tongue, the bitterness of the powder made me want to vomit. Here I was lying in a bed in the guest room. Brielle laid across the bottom, and Del sat in a chair in the corner. The pain that was going through my body, I would wish on nobody. The cramps were intense, and I felt like I was being ripped apart. I flinched a bit, but I didn't yell out. The tears rolled down my face as I said a little prayer in my head wishing this shit would be over soon.

Brielle's face wore a look of sadness.

"You good?" she asked.

I simply nodded my head, even though I was lying. The energy in the room was depressing.

"I'm going to head into the other room so that I can take a nap," Brielle whispered.

When Brielle left the room, Del put his phone down and climbed in bed beside me. The way I felt I didn't even want to be touched, but I welcomed his compassion.

"Do you regret doing this? It was your child too?" he asked, shocking me.

"Would I be a bad person if I said hell no? I don't want any kids right now, and I most definitely don't want to be tied down to NaQuan. I know what I meant to tell you. Give me my phone," I told him.

Del reached over and grabbed my phone, handing it to me. Maneuvering through my phone, I found the voice recording and pressed play. The recording of the confession replayed, and I watched as Del tensed up.

"Yo, what you gone do with that?" he asked. I shrugged my shoulders because I didn't know.

"I guess when the time comes, or he tries to do something to me, I could use it as leverage over his head, and he'll leave me alone."

"That nigga ain't finna leave you alone. You told him you were pregnant, Lace. You gone tell him you got an abortion?" he asked.

All the questions were becoming too much, and I didn't want to talk about it as another pain hit me hard.

"Let me take this one day at a time. I can't do it right now." I sighed.

———

Monday evening had come, and I had just returned from Brielle's house. The first night we stayed at Del's, but after that, we went back to Brielle's so that no one would grow suspicious. There wasn't any school today, but I had to return tomorrow and continue on with my life.

When I entered the house, I was trying to look as normal as possible so that nobody would think anything. When I walked into the house, my dad was sitting on the couch cleaning his boots.

"Hey, daddy!" I spoke, trying to sound chipper.

"Hey, baby girl. You have a good weekend?" he asked.

"Yes, really didn't do much but stay in the house," I answered. He nodded his head and returned to his boots.

Making my way upstairs, I headed to my room and started to put up my things. The extra pack of pads I had I took them and placed them in my drawer. Removing my shoes, I changed into something more comfortable and climbed in my bed. As soon as I grabbed the remote to turn my TV on, there was a knock on my door.

"What?" I called out because I wasn't about to get out the bed.

My door was unlocked anyway. The door slowly opened, and I glanced over my shoulder. NaQuan stepped in quietly. I didn't have time for this boy shit.

"How my baby doing?" he laughed.

"Ain't no, baby," I proudly responded. Now he was standing at the foot of my bed.

"What the fuck you mean, Lace?" he spat.

"Oh, I killed that shit." I shrugged. NaQuan jumped on the bed and grabbed me.

"You did what?" he yelled, spit hitting me in my face.

"You really thought I was about to have a kid and on top of that by you? I had an abortion, and thank you for paying for it," I smirked.

"If your daddy wasn't downstairs, I'll beat the shit out of you for that dumb shit. That was my seed! I knew your ass stole from me."

"Get out of my room, NaQuan, because I'm this close to calling the police on you. The next time you put your hands on me in any kind of way, you going to jail, and I'm telling everybody about what you been doing," I spoke with so much confidence.

"Ain't nobody gone believe you. That shit your word against mine." He laughed.

"You remember that conversation we had when you came in here asking me about your money. I recorded everything. Also, I already sent copies to two other phones in case you try to do something like break my phone or whatever. Get up and don't step foot in my room for nothing else," I said.

NaQuan had a surprised yet disheartening look on his face, but I could tell he was weighing his options. Slowly he climbed off me and walked out of my room.

Chapter Fifteen

DELMAZIO

Things had been moving so fast once things were back on schedule. Ever since Lace's abortion, she had been freer and more outspoken. She came back to school as if nothing ever happened. What I did notice was that NaQuan was always mad as hell now. Every time he saw me, he would give me the deadliest look. It was senior week, and after the big game tomorrow, my homie was having the biggest party of the year.

Walking through the halls, I headed to the gym to change for practice.

"Del!" Coach called out as I walked past his office.

"Wassup, Coach?" I answered, putting my head in the door.

"Come in, son, let me holler at you," he answered. Walking in, I took a seat in the chair in front of his desk.

"Now you know Friday these game scouts will be in attendance. I have put in a few good words with some of the top recruiters, but I don't want to put any pressure on you. Just go out there and play like you do any other game," he told me.

"I appreciate that, Coach," I said, standing up to leave.

"Get ya head in the game and off them females. There's nothing wrong with love, but it holds you by the balls when you least expect it," he smirked.

All I did was shake my head because one thing I knew about Lace was we were going to be alright. I headed on to the locker room and got my head right for practice.

————

Later that night, I laid in bed, staring at the ceiling trying to keep a clear head for tomorrow's game. This was important, and I couldn't mess it up at all because all the recruits were going to be there, and I needed all the good. This game was going to help the outcome of my life.

My phone buzzed, and I turned over grabbing it off the nightstand. Looking at the screen it was Lace. I answered, and her smiling face graced the screen.

"Sup, baby?" I asked. She tucked her hair behind her ear and smiled at me. I could tell she was blushing.

"I missed you today. How was practice?" she asked.

"It was cool. A nigga's just trying to focus since the recruits will be out at the game tomorrow. Coach told me to get my head in the game." I sighed.

"Well, you have to do what you have to do, baby, and I'm going to be in the stands cheering for you. We will get our time tomorrow after the game. Are you picking me up for the party?" She lifted her brow.

"Yeah, I'll scoop you from Brielle's," was all I said.

"Cool, Goodnight, boo."

"Goodnight," I said and ended the call.

It made me want Lace more the way that she didn't act a way because I might have been neglectful or standoffish. She knew it wasn't anything personal, but it was about my future. I could rock with shorty forever off the strength of that alone.

Chapter Sixteen

LACE

The yells from the crowd were so loud that I had to step out the bleachers. We had beat East school, and Del showed his ass off tonight. The feeling that I felt for him was that of joy after a huge accomplishment. I stood off to the side outside of the double doors as they all walked off the court. When I saw him wink at me, my heart melted. A few men were standing off to the side as well, and they greeted Del and shook his hand. I figured they were the recruiters that he was talking about. I was in no hurry because I knew this was important to him.

Brielle walked over after wrapping it up with the cheer-leaders. Her bouncy curls were bouncing as she skipped over.

"You ready to get ready for this party?" she asked.

"Yeah, I just wanted to say something to Del first," I told her, nodding over to him.

It looked like the conversation was wrapping up because he went in for a hug of one of the men. After they walked off, he made his way over to me, dropping his towel and scooping me off my feet.

"Them boys just offered me a full ride. They told me to think about it?" he shouted.

"Where were they from?" I asked.

"Alabama State. Shit, a nigga's ready to turn up, though. Come on." He grabbed my hand as we headed to the car.

During the entire ride to Brielle's house, I was silent. I knew that when he went off to college, it was a chance of us being separated, so all this was hitting me at once. I was happy for him, but I was scared at the thought of losing him. Will we be able to stay together with a long-distance relationship? Will our love for one another fade? Who will protect me from NaQuan if he decides to start back up with his bullshit?

We pulled up outside of Brielle's, and Del turned the radio down. Brielle stepped out of the car, and I turned to look at him.

"What's bothering you, Lace? You've been quiet the whole ride home." Del sighed.

"Nothing, baby, I'm just thinking about what may happen to us whenever you decide to go off to college," I truthfully answered.

Del pushed his hair out of his face and ran his hand over it.

"We're going to work out wherever I go. Whatever I decide to do, it will be for both of us. I'm not going to leave you high and dry, so stop stressing about that. Go in there, get ready, and call me when you ready for me to scoop y'all back up," he said, reassuring me.

It sounded good for the time being, but we shall see.

———

It took about an hour for Brielle and me to get ready because it was now ten p.m., and the party was already popping from people Snapchat stories and IG posts. Del was in route while Brielle and I finished flat ironing my hair.

"I think Del and I might leave the party early," I smirked.

"Nasty ass girl, I hope y'all using protection. We don't need no accidents." Brielle looked at me, lifting her brow.

"I wouldn't dare fuck up his life like that. I'm not ready for no damn kids' period." I laughed.

Running the comb over my leave out, I was ready to go. Grabbing my jacket, we headed downstairs and outside because Del was pulling up.

When I got in the car, he handed me a lit blunt that he had been smoking on, I took a couple of tokes and felt at ease. The sounds of Jeezy were coming out of the speakers, and I was feeling it. Passing the blunt to Brielle in the back-seat, I started rapping along to "Lose My Mind".

About fifteen minutes later, we pulled up at the party. It was held at one of Del's team member's house. Cars were lined up and down both sides of the street and in the yard. My dad would shit a brick if we parked in his grass. Brielle hopped out the car so fast, and Del and I walked in hand in hand. Everyone was cheering for him when he walked in like he was that nigga, all I did was smile.

"I'm about to go grab something to drink," I pulled Del towards me to whisper in his ear.

Walking through the thick crowd, all eyes were on me. These hoes couldn't stand me since Del and I got together. They already didn't like me, but when the word got out, they really hated me.

Walking over to the punch bowl, I poured me something that was already mixed, and the liquor amount was excessive because I could smell it, and it was that strong.

"Where's NaQuan at?" I turned around and ran dead smack into one of his friends. Irritation etched on my face, and I rolled my eyes.

"I don't keep up with him and prefer not to even hear his name," I replied and walked off. I prayed like hell he didn't show up at this party, but with him being a senior as well, I knew luck wasn't on my side.

As I walked off, I gulped the drink in my hand down and made my way back to Del. "She Will" by Lil Wayne came on, and I lost my shit. I bent over and started slow twerking on Del. The vibe in here was everything, and Brielle came through with the twerk on one of Del's friends. When the song ended, we laughed it off and continued to enjoy the night. I was on drink number two, and I wasn't sure if it was the liquor or what, but my stomach started feeling queasy.

"You good?" Del asked as he pulled me into his lap. Leaning back against his chest, I nodded my head yeah. I didn't want to worry him because I wasn't ready to leave. The night was just getting started. That's when our eyes met. The frown that he wore on his face caused me to tense up immediately, and I prayed that things didn't get out of hand. NaQuan made his way through the crowd, and he never stopped looking at me.

"Don't let that nigga get to you. He ain't finna say shit to you if I got anything to do with it!" Del spat.

"I'm cool, let's dance," I suggested.

The pace had slowed down, and Kelly Rowland's "Motivation" was playing in the background. Placing my hands around his neck, I let my hands roam through his curly bun, something that I did all the time. Del put his face closer to mine and licked his sexy lips.

"You just out here thotting it up, ain't ya?" NaQuan spat.

That feeling that I had in the pit of my stomach increased. I slowly turned around to face Naquan, and his eyes were low. I knew he was high. His sidekicks were standing on the side of him.

"NaQuan, please leave me alone. I'm not bothering you,"

was all I managed to muster up.

"You ain't got to be bothering me, but you in here showing your ass with this nigga is gone get you fucked up!" he spat.

Del moved me out the way and made his way in NaQuan's face.

"You know this little fetish/crush thing you got going on for Lace needs to stop. I bet y'all thought this nigga was just being the protective big brother, but nah, this nigga got a thang for his sister." Del laughed. I felt lower than low and didn't want everyone in my business.

"Del, just leave it alone, please," I begged.

At this point, they were standing so close their noses were touching, so I placed my arm in between the both of them to hopefully stop this shit.

"This is why you killed my baby because you let this bitch ass nigga get in your head with your hoe ass!" NaQuan yelled.

I wanted to crawl in the corner and hide because now everyone was whispering and looking at us strangely.

"Now you're telling lies, NaQuan. Just go home," I cried, trying to flip it as if he was lying.

NaQuan shoved me out the way. Following that, Del hit him with a mean right hook, sending him stumbling back. I was sure that he would lose his footing, but NaQuan came back. Both of them started tussling on the floor, and all I could do was cry.

"Y'all stop them!" I yelled to their friends, but the motherfuckers had pulled out their phones and started recording.

The next thing you know, two loud pops that I knew were gunshots rang out, and instantly everyone started scattering like roaches. NaQuan flew back and hit the floor holding his stomach or chest. I couldn't tell because my eyes were fixed on Del still on the floor holding the smoking gun. Lord, Jesus, shit was about to hit the fan.

Chapter Seventeen

DELMAZIO

Nobody knew that I was strapped, but I didn't go anywhere without a pistol because niggas were crazy out here these days. I intended to come to the party and have a good time with my girl, but NaQuan knows how to get under a nigga skin. I can admit that I let my emotions get the best of me because I didn't mean to air Lace business out like that, but I couldn't believe he mentioned the baby shit.

While we were on the floor tussling, he never saw me reaching for the gun. Nothing could stop me, and when I pulled that trigger, the only thing on my mind was to kill or be killed. Plus, just maybe Lace could finally get some peace in her life. I sat there with my adrenaline still at an all-time high holding the gun. Lace ran over to him screaming while the crimson color of blood filled his shirt and the floor underneath him.

"Oh my god! Someone call the police!" I heard another voice scream from the side of me, and it was Brielle.

"Del, what were you thinking?" Lace spat as she shook me out of my zone. No words left my mouth.

"My nigga, you need to get up out of here before the cops

get here," I heard someone say, and I didn't even know who it was.

"No, he doesn't. It was self-defense!" Lace cried.

The sirens could be heard in the distance, and I knew they would be here fast because of the neighborhood we were in. It was like the closer they got, the slower everything happened. The paramedics rushed in and started working on NaQuan. The nigga was still breathing. I could see the cops in my face, and their lips were moving, but I couldn't hear shit they were saying. The next thing you know, I was jerked up and placed in handcuffs.

Brielle held Lace as she cried her eyes out as the cops walked me out of the house. A crowd had formed outside, and I lifted my head. I wasn't about to hold my head down in defeat. It is what it is, and I would do that shit all over again.

The officer opened the door and pushed my head down so that I could get in the car. Once the door closed, I laid my head against the window and placed my eyes on Lace. Lifting my head, I signaled for her to keep her head held high. She touched her heart, and I was taken to the precinct.

————

Sitting in this small ass room, I had my arms inside my shirt because it was cold as hell in here. They hadn't even given a nigga my one phone call yet. The door opened and in walked a black detective. He gave me a smirk and placed his notepad on the table.

"Alright son, care to explain to me what happened tonight and why NaQuan Kane is in the hospital fighting for his life?" he asked. I looked up at him and took my arms out of my shirt.

"I've been dating NaQuan's sister Lace. He has always been protective of her in a weird way, and she confided in me how he rapes her and shit and be beating on her. Recently, she had gotten pregnant, and we helped her get an abortion."

"Who is we?"

"My mom and her friend Brielle. Anyway, so tonight he comes to the party and starts spazzing out on her. When he shoved her, we got into a fight. I saw him reaching into his pocket, so I grabbed my gun and shot him first." I shrugged.

"There was no gun recovered off of him."

"I don't know what he was reaching for, but I wasn't about to find out. It was either him or me," I told the detective.

"Your mother is outside. She gave us permission to talk to you. Your story does match witness testimony, but once your lawyer gets here, he can explain more to you," he told me before gathering his things.

Chapter Eighteen

LACE

Everything happened so fast once they took Del away. Then I had to do the unthinkable and call my dad because we were minors and telling him that and that NaQuan had been shot was not going well. My face was stained from crying, and my hair was unkempt. Looking at my shoes, they were stained with NaQuan's blood. Doris and my dad were in the back while they did surgery on him. No one had said two words to me, but I knew it was coming. Was I wrong for hoping that he died? NaQuan had hurt me so much that I felt like he got what he deserved.

Looking at the footsteps that were drawing close to me, my father wore a look of pain on his face.

"Let's step outside," was all he said as he passed me.

I got up slowly and followed him out of the double doors. Standing beside me, he looked out into the darkness and took a deep breath before turning to me.

"As my child, I know you may have not been truthful with me about a lot of things, but right now isn't the time. What the fuck happened at that party Lace Monae, and you better fucking tell me everything?" he spat.

"We were at the party having a good time, and NaQuan pops up starting stuff with Del. He was saying some pretty nasty things about me, and Del confronted him, and they got into a scuffle. In the midst of them fighting, Del shot him."

"Why would NaQuan be saying nasty things about you, Lace? It's something you're not telling me. I know you've been messing around with that boy. NaQuan told me that much."

"That's the problem. You believe everything he tells you and thinks that he can't do no wrong when you are so blinded about the things that been going on under your own roof!" I cried. My father squinted his eyes and looked at me.

"NaQuan is your brother. He is your protector. So what are you saying?" he asked.

"That's it. He isn't my brother. NaQuan is fucking sick, and ever since he moved in, he's been raping and beating on me every damn day. His protective ways aren't because he's being a brother. It's because this man thinks we can have a whole relationship. When you and Doris go to your room at night, you have no idea the things I go through. He's been speaking ill on Del because he doesn't want anybody to have me. The whole fight ensued because Del called him out in front of everybody at the party. Then NaQuan flipped it and brought up the abortion," I mumbled the last part.

My father grabbed me.

"What fucking abortion?" he yelled, spit hitting me in my face.

"I had gotten pregnant by NaQuan, so I stole some money from him and got an abortion. He knew about it, and if you don't believe any of this, I got everything recorded on my phone," I said, pulling my phone out and quickly pulling up the conversation. I held the phone out so my father could hear, and it was like he grew horns.

"Why you didn't tell me this sooner? Dammit, Lace, I'm

your father, not his. There is no way I wouldn't have taken this shit serious!" he yelled. Folks were bypassing us, walking into the waiting room.

"You and he had this whole father/ son relationship going that I honestly didn't think you would believe me. Remember when you ask me if I having sex and I told you yes. I was, but not with Del. I was speaking in circles. That's why I never wanted to be around him. That boy is crazy. I know what Del did may not seem right, daddy, but he was protecting me. He and Brielle were the only ones that knew what was going on," I admitted.

My father looked different. The anger in him was showing. I reached out and grabbed his arm.

"Dad, what are you thinking?" I asked. When I saw a tear slide down his cheek and his fist balled up, I wasn't sure what was about to happen.

"Arrrgh!" he yelled out in frustration.

"Do you know how it feels that I couldn't do shit to protect my daughter? This whole time I had this boy in my house. This nigga got what he deserves, and I wish his mammy would say a motherfucking thing!" he snapped.

"I'm fine, daddy. Let's just wait and see what happens then we can go from there," I told him.

"This is all your fault!" Doris came charging at me out the doors.

"You better step off of her!" My daddy grabbed her.

"My son is in there clinging on for his life all because he tried to protect you from that bum ass boy you been dating. The detective told me.

"Well, the detective must not have told you the entire truth because your rapist ass son was too busy telling the world how he got me pregnant."

"Bitch, what did you say?"

Doris came charging after me again, but I inched closer to

her because I wanted her to hit me with all the anger I had in me I was gone knock her old ass out.

"Now wait a damn minute. What you not gone do is come down here and point fingers when you don't know the whole story. After the shit I just was told, that nigga deserves to be laying up there!" my dad spat.

Doris' eyes widened.

"Why in the hell would she be calling my son a rapist?" she asked.

"Because that's all he been doing to me since y'all moved in," I replied.

"Girl, please! You were probably just being a hot ass, and now that it done came out, you crying rape."

"Play the motherfucking tape!" my dad demanded.

Retrieving my phone, I played the recording, and Doris looked embarrassed. She didn't even have any words. She just turned and walked off.

"Yeah, that's what I thought. I'll deal with you later," he told Doris and turned to me.

"Look, go home and get cleaned up. Don't you talk to nobody, you hear me?" I nodded my head and waited for him to hand me his keys.

My heart went out to my father because I knew he was hurting and couldn't take his anger out on the one he needed to. Then there was Del. Oh my god, I wonder what he was enduring in jail.

Chapter Nineteen

MONTE

Walking back inside the hospital, it was a million things on my brain. At this moment I wasn't a husband, stepdaddy, or none of that shit. My flesh and blood were my priority. Do you know how it feels to hear the pain from your child and you weren't able to do anything? I can't believe this whole time all this was going on underneath my nose.

When I stepped back on the floor, Doris sat in the waiting area crying. This was still my wife, the woman I had married and took vows with.

"Any update?" I asked, taking my seat beside her.

"Not that you care, but it's touch and go," she mumbled.

"You're right about that. I don't mean to sound cold, but as a parent, I wasn't able to protect my child from that monster of a son of yours. Did you know what he was doing?" I asked her.

"Hell no, and I still think we will never know the whole truth behind it until he recovers."

"Well, I believe my child, just like you got that belief in yours that he didn't do that shit. My child was fucking pregnant by him for Pete's sake. He was obsessed with her, and I trusted him with her. Honestly, Doris, I don't know where we stand after this because I don't want him back in my house," I said as I stood up.

"Kane family," a doctor called out. When Doris stood to greet him, I stayed back a little.

"Is my son ok?" she asked.

"I'm Dr. Barnes as you know NaQuan was brought in with a gunshot wound to the torso and chest. We had our entire trauma unit working diligently during surgery, but it seems the bullet traveled once inside, and we were unsuccessful with our treatments. I'm sorry to say that he didn't make it. We did everything possible to save your son," he told her, and Doris fell to the floor, yelling to the top of her lungs. I nodded my head to the doctor, and he walked off.

Bending down, I pulled Doris towards my chest and consoled her. Then she started to punch me.

"Get off me! This is what you wanted! You happy now?" she screamed. I knew she was hurting, but I stood up. No words left my mouth.

"Leave!" she yelled. Turning on my heels, I did just that.

Chapter Twenty

LACE

It had been three weeks since NaQuan's murder. The energy in the house was different because my father was sulking. I knew it wasn't because of NaQuan, but because he had lost the woman he loved. I didn't attend school for a week because I was embarrassed by everything that had transpired. Even though I was the victim, I just wasn't ready to face everyone seeing that they didn't even care for me anyway.

Del's mother had hired him a pretty good lawyer, but I haven't had the chance to talk to him. His lawyer did speak to the attendees at the party as well as me, and everyone's story was the same. I even gave him the recording so that he could use it in court as a motive for the fight and to further prove that NaQuan was raping me. Doris moved all of her things out of the house and swore up and down her son was still innocent. I knew the truth, and I was glad that he was dead.

News traveled fast, and once my mom caught wind of it, she called a million times a day. I missed my mother so much. She even threatened to have Doris touched from the inside. After finishing my work, I packed it up neatly so that Brielle could get it when she swung by. Once I had everything packed up, I pulled out my phone and laid across the couch watching damn daytime TV.

The sound of the mailman pulling up caught my attention. Swinging my feet off the couch, I slid my feet in my slides and headed to get the mail.

Walking outside, I walked to the mailbox and retrieved the mail scanning through all the envelopes when my eyes landed on a name I wasn't expecting to see. Quickly I pulled the envelope close to me, making sure that I wasn't tripping. It was a letter from Del. I ran in the house and closed the door, tossing the mail on the table. Ripping the letter open, I just stared at it blankly. I was scared to read. I didn't know what this was even though I was thrilled to hear from him.

Tangled Lace

I know you are probably wondering why I called you that. I just want to apologize for making your life a chaotic mess. Yeah, I know what I did was to protect you, but it just added to what you were going through. It's only been a few weeks in here, but behind these walls, it feels like forever. I don't regret a thing, though. I would do it all over again. Look, though. I wrote you to let you know that if things do go as planned, I'll be able to get out, but I won't be returning to Nashville. Everybody withdrew their scholarships due to the shit that happen, so a nigga is going to live with my uncle. Maybe it wasn't really meant for me to play basketball after all.

Of course, I will stay in touch, but I told my mother to tell you about the court date in case you want to attend. Lace Monae, you were everything I ever wanted and needed. Even with your flaws, you made me complete. If I could take all the pain that you ever endured away, I would. I want you to move forward in your life. Who knows, things might work out for the both us if it's meant to be. I want you to go on to do great things, but I'm going to be good and will beat this. I love you girl, forever

Delmazio

Once I finished reading, I glanced at it repeatedly, just

reading it. What was he saying? Did he really want to end us? I knew why. Our future was unpredictable right now, not knowing the outcome and if we even had a future. I never thought Delmazio would tell me he loved me, but the feeling was mutual.

Closing the letter, I placed it back in the envelope and set it on the table. Letting out a deep sigh, I closed my eyes and just prayed for him and for peace to be restored in both of our lives. The ringing of the doorbell brought me out of my prayer, and I headed to the door.

Thinking it was Brielle, I opened it without looking out first. When I opened the door, I got the shock of my life. I hadn't seen the person standing in front of me in forever. It was like all the emotions came flooding back. My heart started to pound, and my armpits began to sweat.

"What are you doing here?" I asked. A smile graced their face.

"I'm back for good, and I heard about everything, so I was checking on you," he said.

"Juan, I appreciate it, but you're the last person I want to see," I lied.

Damn, I used to love this nigga. Seeing him standing here looking finer than ever as if he matured while he was gone had me forgetting everything that just happened.

"You sure about that?" he asked, opening his arms, gesturing for a hug. He walked closer to me, and I couldn't move. Falling into his arms felt right and came too easy.

EIGHT YEARS LATER

Chapter Twenty-One

LACE

"Lace five minutes before it's time for you to go out there," Brielle said as she walked back in the room.

I sat here staring in the mirror, thinking about all the events that led me to this day. Today my life would change forever. It was my wedding day and my 24th birthday. Let's just say things changed with me over the course of eight years.

"Brielle, I don't think I can do this," I mumbled. Brielle walked over to me as she put her earrings in her ear.

"What the hell is your problem, you wanted this?" She sighed in irritation.

Easing up from the vanity, I walked over to the enormous glass window of the penthouse and looked out over the city. The only thing on my mind was how much my life had changed.

"I know I want this, but I can't believe this is happening. I would say it happened rather fast, but I guess eight years doesn't really make it that way, huh?" I sighed.

"Well, believe it bitch because in about twenty minutes, your last name will change, and you will be set for life." Brielle smiled.

All that sounded good, but a piece of me still felt bad.

"Come on. It's time to head downstairs," Brielle called out. Giving myself a once-over, we headed out the suite and to the elevators. I could feel Brielle staring a hole in the side of my face.

"What now?" was all I said, not taking my eyes from the elevator doors.

"Have you told him about the baby yet?" she mumbled. Rolling my eyes, the doors opened, and we stepped on the elevator.

"No, why the hell you mention that? I have enough on my mind as it is?" I blew out in frustration. See, this was the thing I was trying to place in the back of my head on my wedding day because I didn't know who the father of my child was. Things took off from that moment Juan showed up on my doorstep. He filled that void that I had from missing Del. You already know that Juan was my first love, from us meeting in middle school and dating until our first year when he left Nashville.

Delmazio was released approximately three months after his trial was completed. His lawyer was that good to get his charged dismissed due to self-defense. Del did what he said and moved to Memphis. They allowed him to complete his probation there. Del and I drifted apart because, I admit, Juan had my mind gone. We kept in touch over the years. Juan had started hustling when he came back to Nashville and had made a name for himself. My entire senior year flew by, and it was one of the happiest years of my life. When I graduated, we moved in together, and he has been taking care of me ever since. I attended Cosmetology school and eventually made hair my passion.

Fast forward to a year ago when I found out Juan had cheated on me. That had done something to me because I thought we were better than that. It's obvious the more money made, the more problems followed. When I found out about his infidelity, I hit Del up, and we sort of became dependent on one another with our problems. I would come to him, and he would come to me. He started filling the voids I was getting from Juan. Juan knows all about Del's and my relationship and history, so he doesn't like him at all. He won't admit it, but I think he sees Del as a problem when it comes to my heart, and that's why I feel he rushed this marriage.

Juan and I had a huge argument, two months ago, I went to Memphis to spend the weekend with Del, and of course, it got hot the whole weekend between the two of us. Now, we're here. Neither Juan nor Del knows I'm pregnant, and if Juan ever finds out I had sex with Del, he would kill my ass.

"Lace, look. I know you don't want to talk about it, but what are you going to do?" Brielle asked. I held my head down as the tears started to flow.

"I don't know Brielle, but I have this gut feeling that it belongs to Juan. I'm going to tell him soon enough, okay?" I reassured her and patted my eyes with the cloth that I had in my hand.

The elevator came to a stop, and we got off headed towards the ballroom. Walking down the hall, I spotted the wedding planner signaling for me to hurry. I had the sudden urge to vomit hit me, but I brushed it off and placed the biggest grin on my face.

"Hey, baby girl," my father greeted me.

My eyes shifted to behind him, and I felt heat all over my body as Del walked in with some bitch on his arm. Who the fuck invited him? See, now he was playing a dangerous game.

"You okay? You look like you just saw a ghost?" my father asked. Little did he know I did.

"I'm fine, just a little tired, that's all." I smiled. Brielle caught my eye and shook her head when she saw what I was looking at.

"Fuck him, it's your time," she said as she prepared to walk in the church.

The music started, and I stood arm in arm with my dad as my girl made her way down the aisle. Walking towards the entrance, the door closed, and it was now or never, no turning back. When the doors opened again, and I laid eyes on Juan standing there looking so happy, I started to panic. On cue, the music started and my father and I made our way down the aisle.

Oh my god, how could I do this to Juan? Hell, he cheated on me, so maybe he will understand. Hell no, he won't understand anything dealing with Del. All these thoughts were running through my head. As I got closer, I started to feel as if all the air in the room had shut off and the room began to spin.

BLAM!

Chapter Twenty-Two

JUAN PRICE

Looking over at Lace at her hooked up in this hospital bed was fucking with me. One minute I'm about to get married, and then the next minute, I'm not. Lace has been my rider since the moment I came back in her life. I couldn't ask for a better person to share the rest of my life with. I was born in Brooklyn, New York but when I turned one my parents relocated to Louisville, Kentucky. I spent most of my life there until moms divorced my pops and she moved to Nashville.

When I came to Nashville, I was in the fifth grade. Not knowing anyone, I met Brielle and Lace because Lace had the hots for a nigga. We kicked it off and started dating until our freshman year of high school. Being with someone that long, the feelings we had for one another just didn't go away when I left.

I hated to leave Nashville, but I went back to Louisville to stay with my pops. The laws in Kentucky weren't made for a young black boy, so I was constantly in trouble because I wanted the streets. When I decided to come back to Nashville, I had my mind set on getting my girl back, and that's what I did. I admit it was hard at first because while I was gone Lace went through so much shit that I couldn't believe my ears. Then she admitted that she was partly in love with another dude.

Now, I know I did my fair share of shit over the years, and Lace stood by a nigga and never stepped out on me, but she had secrets. I could tell she was getting tired though, so I figured marriage would make her happier. I admit I was a popping ass nigga, and I held weight. My appearance and money were what Lace hated so much because the women that followed. I've always been a nice looking nigga, but once I took control of my weight and focused on my health, my body was one that the ladies loved. My yellow skin was so marked up with tattoos that I couldn't even tell you how many I had.

"Where am I?" Lace groggily asked, looking around. I walked over towards the hospital bed.

"Try not to move too much. You're in the hospital. You passed out walking down the aisle," I explained, rubbing her hair out of her face.

The door to her room opened, and in came Brielle carrying plates of food.

"Oh my god, you're finally up!" she squealed, placing the plates down and making her way to the bed.

"How long have I been here?" Lace asked.

"Three days," I told her.

A strange look graced her face, and she fell silent. There was another knock on the door, and the nurse entered carrying a huge flower arrangement.

"Sorry to interrupt, but someone left these for you," she said. I walked towards her.

"I'll take those." I grabbed the flowers and placed them on the window seal.

"Who are they from?" both Brielle and Lace asked while Brielle made her way over to me.

Grabbing the card out the flowers, I read it. The rage that overcame me had me seeing red. I reached for the flowers and tossed them shits in the trash.

"Maybe Lace can tell me!" I spat, throwing the card in her face.

"Whoa now, what the fuck is your problem?" Brielle snapped. Lace grabbed the card and read it.

"Lace, baby, I miss you and what we had. Hope you okay. Love you Del," I quoted what was on the card in a mocking tone. Lace couldn't do shit but hold her head down.

"I'm going to leave you two alone," Brielle said and exited the room fast as hell. I couldn't even look at Lace's ass.

Walking over to the window, I held my head down because a nigga was hurt. Maybe I was overthinking shit, but knowing her secret too, what if I wasn't tripping?

"What the fuck was that all about, Lace? You been fucking around on me and with all people Del? I ought to choke the shit out of you right here in this goddamn hospital. All of a sudden you being real sneaky about a lot of shit. Lace, when were you going to tell me about the baby?" I yelled.

Yeah, the doctor had informed my ass, and all this time, I couldn't see why Lace ain't tell me. She knew I wanted kids.

"I wanted to tell you, Juan. I just didn't know how," she said, crying. Them tears didn't mean a damn thing to me. Lace could save that shit.

"Bullshit, Lace, you know how bad I wanted kids, so what you mean you ain't know how to tell me? Maybe you didn't tell me because your trifling ass doesn't know who the father is!" I spat with so much venom. I knew it shocked her due to her facial expression.

"Juan, you have a right to be mad, but didn't you cheat on me with Lovey?" she had the nerve to say. I marched over towards her, and she picked up the nurse call button as if she was scared.

"That was over a year ago, Lace. You're damn near two months, so that means you been cheating recently. I've been doing right by you. How long you been back fucking that nigga Del?" I asked not even sure if I wanted to know the answer.

Lace let out a sigh.

"It's not even what you think. When Brielle and I took that trip to Memphis, we ran into each other at the club, and I was drinking heavily, and we hooked up. I'm sorry I didn't tell you this sooner. I was planning on getting an abortion, but I feel deep down inside that this is your child, Juan," she admitted.

Man, I wanted to jump Lace's ass in this bed. This type of shit I expected from these hoes out here in the streets trying to trap a nigga, but not from the one girl that I had damn near grew up with. I should've left her ass alone when she told me she still had love for that nigga. I should've known better. This shit hurt coming from her in the worst way, and I might even regret what I was about to say.

"Well, Lace you killed us, I'm glad you fell out at the wedding because you stopped a nigga from making a huge mistake. You can stay at the house and keep your car because I ain't that grimy, but it's over, boo," I told her. Reaching for my things, I took one last look at Lace and walked the fuck out.

Chapter Twenty-Three

LACE

Three Months Later

The ringing of my cell phone woke me from my slumber. Looking at the clock, I saw it was 7:45 a.m. I slowly grabbed the phone and placed it on speaker.

"Hello," I answered, voice raspy and everything.

"Bitch, I know you ain't still sleep, and you got to be at your ultrasound at 8:30? I'm coming in the house, so get your ass up!" Brielle yelled in the phone.

All I did was shake my head. Today was the day that I found out the sex of my baby. That day Juan left out the hospital hurt me, and I cried for two weeks straight until Brielle had to get in my ass. I realized I was wrong for letting my heart get me into this mess. I wasn't about to force him if he didn't want me or to be apart this child's life. I hadn't heard or seen from him since. Del kept trying to reach out, but I wasn't answering him either. I was just focused on my baby and me.

Brielle came storming in the room, and I took off towards the bathroom to get me a quick shower because I didn't want to hear her mouth.

"You better run!" she yelled.

Starting the shower, I hopped in and took me a quick one. Rubbing over my protruding belly, I glanced down and smiled. The joy that I had of the thoughts of being a mother was everything. I never thought I would be pregnant again after the abortion I had with NaQuan's baby when I was a teen, but God blessed me.

Rinsing off, I stepped out of the shower and took care of my face and mouth hygiene. Exiting the bathroom, Brielle laid across my bed, eyes glued to her phone. Next to her were my clothes.

"Brielle, are you dressing me now?" I asked. Looking at the outfit, I didn't complain. I just started to get dressed.

"Time is ticking, so I just decided to help out hush," she answered.

Once I was dressed and ready, we both headed out.

———

When we finally arrived at the doctor's, we were a tad late, but we made it. After checking in, Brielle and I both took out seats. Scanning the room my eyes landed on this couple sitting across the room. The happiness that was etched on their faces made me think of Juan.

"What's wrong, Lace?" Brielle whispered in my ear.

"I always thought this moment I would spend with Juan," I said dryly. Brielle never talked about Juan when I mentioned him because she was still pissed at him for walking out on me.

"Lace Tucker," the nurse called me. I tapped Brielle, and we both stood and made our way to the back. Once inside, the nurse got me situated while Brielle took a seat beside me.

"Ok. The doctor will be in shortly." She smiled and walked out of the room. Sitting back on the table, I looked at Brielle. The door opened and in walked Dr. Karen.

"It's so good to see you, Lace. Are you ready to find out the sex of this little munchkin?" She smiled.

"Yes ma'am, more than ready?" I smiled.

Dr. Karen lifted my shirt and applied the cold gel to my abdomen. Gliding the instrument over my stomach, my baby was cutting up, and it was funny to see it moving on the machine.

"Lord, well, whatever it is, it sho is active." She laughed.

"Look right here. It looks like he wants us to see that he will be a ladies man, Lace. It's a boy." Dr. Karen laughed.

"Oh, Lord, another knucklehead." Brielle sighed.

"As long as he's healthy, I don't care what it is," I admitted.

"I would like to see you back in two months, so make a follow-up appointment, and these are yours to keep," Dr. Karen said, handing me the ultrasound print outs.

As she left the room, I got up excited knowing now that I could place a name with my son. We walked out of the doctor's office and a smile etched my face.

"Let's celebrate, how about manis and pedis and have dinner tonight somewhere," I suggested.

"What's came over you? You never want to go out, but if that's what you want, then I'm down," she said.

We hopped in the car and drove to East Nashville to The Nail Bar. I had tried my hardest to avoid this side of town because I knew this was Juan stomping ground at the barbershop next door. I wanted him to see that I was doing great without him. When I whipped into the parking lot, I immediately noticed his truck sitting up front.

"Ain't this a bitch." Brielle laughed and shook her head at me.

"What the fuck is so funny?" I asked.

"What's funny is you. You're ready to face this nigga after all this time. I know you came over here for a reason."

"If I came for a reason, that means I'm ready to face him and show him what the fuck he walked out on," I said.

"Whatever, let's go." Brielle chuckled, and we got out of the car.

When we crossed the parking lot, the doors of the barbershop opened, and one of Juan's friends walked out, and Juan was trailing behind him. This couldn't be happening.

Juan looked good as hell. I could tell he just got out the chair because his beard was nice and trimmed to perfection. The hunter green sweater he was rocking with the matching polo hat look nice against his skin. When our eyes met, he licked his plump lips and showcased his diamond grill. One of his friends had said something to him because he started laughing.

"Sup, Lace?" his homeboy Trey spoke. Trey and I have always been cool.

"Hey, Trey, wassup?" I happily answered as we made our way towards the nail salon.

"Damn, girl, you getting out there. You know what you having yet?" he asked.

"As a matter of fact, I do. We just left the doctor. It's a boy," I said, looking over at Juan, making sure he heard me. To my surprise, he was smiling.

"That's wassup. Let me know the details so I can get the little nigga something," Trey said.

"I will, but excuse us. We got to go get cute so we can celebrate tonight." I laughed and opened the door to the salon.

"Be careful, shorty!" Juan called out.

"She will!" Brielle snapped.

Chapter Twenty-Four

BRIELLE

I knew that my girl missed Juan's trifling ass, but she could do without. Honestly, I was team Del anyway. I knew what I was doing was going against the girl code, but I was still in contact with Del. He loved the fuck out of Lace, and we ain't know who's she was carrying. Lace didn't know, but Del had moved back to Nashville a couple of weeks ago.

When we graduated from high school, I went on to college, and my love life was nonexistent. The only thing I wanted to focus on was my studies because I was determined to make something out of myself. Yeah, that shit sounded good, but it didn't last long.

Entering my sophomore year, I met this guy name Diggy. Diggy was the star player of the basketball team. We clicked instantly, and the love was there. Nothing could go wrong, and we were inseparable. That was until one break he decided to stay on campus instead of going home. Well, we got a surprise on his doorstep, when his girlfriend popped up, stomach big as day. I tried to knock his ass out. This man was living two different lives, one on campus, and the other back in his hometown. Diggy hurt me, and I left him.

"Damn, he was fine as hell," Lace said, snapping me out of my thoughts.

"I knew you couldn't resist. Don't fall for that nigga so fast, Lace. Keep in mind he left you hanging three months ago, and you haven't heard from that nigga since," I told her.

"Yeah, that's true, but you have to understand what if this is his child. We gone have to put this shit aside anyway," she mumbled.

"No matter what I say, you gone do what you want anyway, but just remember Juan's been out here for three months doing him. Don't think that nigga done turned Jehovah or some shit." I sighed.

"I'm going to be fine, Brielle. Everybody ain't Diggy," Lace had the nerve to say.

"Fuck you." I rolled my eyes.

Juan

Seeing Lace was something that I needed. I had been avoiding her for quite some time now. With the way she carried herself, I could tell she was doing good. She had a glow about her. Maybe it was the baby. Word around town was that nigga Del had moved back, so I wonder if he had been keeping her company. I mean, yeah, I ain't hit her up since I left the hospital, but she could've always reached out to me like she does when we usually fight.

"Man, nigga, I know you still feeling shorty, and that little nigga in her stomach might be yours." Trey looked at me.

"I know, man, but I haven't talked to Lace since I walked out the hospital and left her there. I love her ass to death. A nigga ain't been with nobody in three months because I want to be with her. She probably will never forgive me after the way I did her," I admitted.

"True that, but considering there is a baby at question y'all might need to have a one-on-one. That gives you time to apologize."

"Why am I the one apologizing when she cheated on me, Trey? I was about to marry her, and she blindsided me the entire time."

"Don't act like you weren't blindsiding her, and you know what I'm talking about. Both of y'all need to quit yo shit and get it together," Trey said.

He was right, and maybe that was why I left because I felt guilty as well, but that shit hurt still. Pulling out my phone, I scrolled to Lace's number and sent her a text.

Me: *Do Del know y'all having a boy?*

Wifey: *Really? You got your nerve texting me this bullshit, but I haven't had any communication with Del. If this baby is his, he won't have anything to do with it. Plus, I know he's yours!!*

After the last text came through, I kept rereading it. I smiled and nodded my head, looking at Trey.

"I think a nigga finna go back home," was all I said.

———

It was about six p.m., and I pulled into the driveway of the home that I used to share with Lace. Sitting here for a few seconds, I prayed like hell that she would welcome me with open arms. I took another hit of the blunt before putting it out in the ashtray. Stepping out the car, I slowly walked up the steps and prayed that the locks were the same. Sticking the key in the door, the knob turned, and I let out a sigh of relief. Entering the house, all the lights were off, and the TV was on in the living room. When I eased over towards the couch, Lace laid there knocked out. She looked so peaceful.

Slowly I moved towards her and placed my hands on her stomach. When I rubbed my hand across, it startled her, causing her to move in her sleep.

"What the hell, Juan?" she spat.

"I didn't mean to scare you," I told her. She scooted up, sitting up on the couch and looked at me with low eyes.

"What are you doing here?" she asked. I got up and sat down on the couch beside her.

"I ain't gonna front a nigga been missing you like crazy. When I saw you today, it was no way that I could continue without fixing this mess between us. The way that I reacted was out of embarrassment and hurt, but I shouldn't have gone by it like that. These last three months have been hell, and I know you might not believe me, but I ain't been fucking with nobody. We both made some fucked-up decisions, and how I see it, we just put them in the past and move on," I said, letting it all out. Lace wiped the tears from her eyes.

"I missed you so much, Juan." Hearing her say that made a nigga smile.

"I missed you too, baby. Come here," I told her, pulling her close to me. When our lips touched, I didn't want to let her go. Damn, I missed this shit so much.

Chapter Twenty-Five

LACE

Letting Juan come back was the best decision I had made. It felt completely different having someone to be by my side during this pregnancy. Yes, Brielle was there, no questions asked, but that wasn't her job, and to have Juan there was a breath of fresh air. He had missed out on so much and was making sure that he didn't miss shit else. Here I was seven months pregnant now, and it was getting harder on my big ass.

My seven-month checkup was today. I looked over at Juan who laid there looking good as hell as he slept. Since he had come back home, my hormones were on ten, and I always wanted sex. Just looking at him now had me turned on.

Lifting the covers, I crawled underneath and removed his dick out of his boxers, placing him in my mouth. I was hesitant at first to go there with him when he first came back home, but he hasn't given me any doubts. Juan started to stir, and when I felt his hand on top of my head, I knew he was enjoying the moment.

Tossing the covers back from off my head, I was really able to get to work. Juan was a nice size, and the thickness of his dick filled my mouth completely. Working my wrist like I was cooking dope in the kitchen, I had him panting like a baby. On count, he was shooting his seeds down my throat, and I held it in my mouth and ran to the bathroom. Laugh all you want. I don't know what it was, but ever since I'd been pregnant, I couldn't swallow that shit. It made me sick.

Spitting his nut in the sink, I brushed my teeth and cleaned my face. Starting the shower, I began to undress and stood in the doorway of the bathroom, looking back at him, he wasn't in bed, I guess he went in the other bathroom. I had a doctor's appointment today, so I didn't have time to play around. The buzzing of his phone caught my attention. I heard it earlier when he was sleep, but I paid it no mind.

Walking over to the nightstand where his phone laid, I saw it was an incoming text. I stood there for a moment, contemplating if I should read it or not. His ass didn't know, but I had been done place my print in his phone. My mind got the best of me, so I picked the phone up. This time it started to ring, and the name Lovey popped up. I knew Lovey, and she knew me because she and Juan had fucked around, so now I was really pissed as to why she was calling his phone.

"Hello," I rudely answered. There was no answer.

"Hello!" I said again. She smacked her lips.

"Can I speak to Juan?" she had the nerve to ask.

"May I ask who's calling?" I replied, fucking with her at this point.

"This is his baby mama, Lovey," she spat. My head flew back, and I looked at the phone, making sure I heard her ass right.

"Who is that on the phone?" Juan asked, making his way over to me. I wanted to smack the shit out of him. I shoved the phone into his chest.

"Your baby mama Lovey," I said calmly. He looked at me face all screwed up.

"What the fuck are you talking about?" he had the nerve to say, but I had walked off in the bathroom and closed the door.

Even though I was listening, I placed my ear against the door to see if I could hear him better.

"Lovey, the fuck you calling my phone for? I ain't talked to your ass in I know two years," he told her. I guess that was good for his ass.

"Man, you straight bugging, I ain't heard from your crazy ass in God knows when, and you call me with that bullshit. Man, do what you got to do!" he yelled and hung up the phone.

She must be trying to pull some slick shit.

I quickly jumped in the shower, and no sooner than I did, the door opened.

"Lace, we need to talk." Juan sighed. I ignored him and kept washing up.

"Lace, I know you hear me!" he spat.

"Whatever you got to say, I don't want to hear it," I said. Grabbing the towel, I wrapped it around my body and got out. I was boiling on the inside.

"Nah, fuck that! When were you going to tell me you had a baby by that nasty ass hoe Lovey? Talking bout she's your baby mama and shit!" I snapped.

Juan made his way over to the bed and sat down.

"Lace, I haven't talked to her since I called it off with her back then. She comes saying I got a son that's about to turn two next month, so I snapped on her because why am I just now hearing of this. Talking about she finna put a nigga on child support if I don't step up, so I told her to do what she had to do." He sighed.

So, that's what the bitch up to. She's always been on that

home-wrecking hoe shit. I walked over to the closet and got my clothes to put on.

"Damn, Lace, say something!" Juan snapped. I whipped my head around so fast.

"What the hell you want me to say, Juan? That I'm cool with it because I'm not. That's something you're gone deal with because if I ever see that bitch again, I'm going to kill her, and that's my word!" I spat and walked out the room.

This shit was stressing me out, and that's the last thing I needed. I couldn't even call Brielle because she was in the Bahamas. Juan was behind me and I acted like he wasn't in the room when I finished getting dressed and got my shoes on. I had a million things running through my head, and I didn't want to put that on my baby.

"What the hell you tripping bout, Lace? I just sat there and told you the truth about the situation? We done made it this far. Come on now," he pleaded.

Yeah, he told me the truth, but how could he expect me to act as if this shit wasn't about to change our world.

"Juan, what if her son is yours? I'm not ready for no outside children. I have one to think about, and that's the one right here," I said, pointing to my big ass belly.

"Lace, you're being selfish. If this is my son, I'm not going to abandon him, and that's that. How I know that's my son you carrying now? Oh, you forgot about Del!" he yelled.

No, the fuck he didn't. He had me fucked up. Grabbing my purse, I walked over to him.

"My nigga, I didn't ask you to come back here and play daddy to mine. You came back on your own. Del is no longer in the picture until I give him a blood test, and you know what, that goes for you too!" I shoved my finger in his head and walked out the door.

I wasn't about to cry over this shit and that toxic ass shit Juan let spew out of his mouth. This nigga was walking around here as if I needed him. I didn't ask him to come back. He wasn't needed, regardless if I missed him or not.

My gas light came on, so I pulled up at the nearest gas station. Hell, I left so fast, I didn't even eat, so I decided to grab a snack as well. Getting out the car, I made my way across the lot when I heard my name. Turning around, I couldn't believe the ghost I was looking at. *Damn, what a motherfucking day.*

Chapter Twenty-Six
DELMAZIO

Moving back to the city was a move I needed to make because my family was here and I missed my mama. Don't get shit twisted. Word gets around, and when I heard Lace was pregnant, there was no way that I was going to be in Memphis if the child turned out to be mine. She was dodging me like the damn plague. Since being back, I done ran into that nigga Juan so many times, and he ain't like a nigga for shit. A nigga like me couldn't care less because he wouldn't dare get out of pocket with a nigga. He would turn his nose up all day on that bitch shit, but he knew to behave. He was a bitch made ass nigga. He thinks he was running shit, but little did he know, he wouldn't be running shit for long.

Sitting at the pump, I was waiting for my sale to pull up when this black Audi whipped in front of me. I reached for my pistol because I didn't know who the fuck it was and the type of bullshit they were on. These motherfuckers up here in the Ville were just as ruthless as the niggas back in Memphis.

When the door opened, my heart sped up. God was on a nigga's side. I rolled the window down

"Lace!" I yelled out, and she turned around. Damn, she was even prettier pregnant. My motherfucking heart. She had a nigga soft like tissue right now. She walked towards the car.

"Tangled Lace, damn, what you been up to?" I smiled.

"Nothing," she said quickly then started to look around. This wasn't my baby girl. I glanced down at her stomach.

"I had heard around the way you were pregnant. How far along are you?" I asked.

"Seven months, look, I got to go." She turned around and walked off. Instantly I hopped out the car and jogged up to her.

"What, Del?" she snapped.

"Shit, you know what I'm about to ask you. Is it mine?" I asked.

"Maybe," she mumbled and jerked away from me.

I had to let that shit register, so I walked back to my car. She really thinks she about to drop some shit like that on me, and I don't react. I watched as she got back in her whip and pulled off. Yeah, call me petty, I pulled off behind her making sure I stayed a few cars back. I had no clue where she was going, but this conversation wasn't over. After everything we done been through, she's treating a nigga like I ain't kill a whole motherfucker for her.

Yeah, I told her to move on, but she knew I still loved her. After fifteen minutes of following her, we pulled up to a doctor's office. She parked her car and pulled behind her. Rolling the window down, I called out to her.

"Are you following me now?" she asked, rolling her eyes.

"Lace, you just dropped a bomb on me back there. How you gone tell me something like that and think I'm just gone leave it at that. You know me better than anyone, so stop playing with me," I told her.

"Look, yeah, it's a possibility that this is your child. When I have him, I'll let you know, and we can do a blood test."

"Lace, stop fucking playing with me. Don't think you about to get rid of me that easy. If that's my child, I'm gone be in his or her life. What does Juan got to say about all this?" I smirked.

"Not that it's any of your business, but he's cool. That bitch Lovey just popped back up after damn near two years saying he got a son that's about to turn two next month." Lace sighed.

I knew about Lovey from around the way because she got around, plus I knew this nigga Lo that she fucked with.

"Word, I just saw that broad at the mall the other day with that nigga Lo."

"Yeah, but look, I'm late for my doctor's appointment. I'm gone hit you up later, okay!" she turned to walk away.

"Lace, would it be too much to ask if I went with you?" I asked, holding my arms in the air. I could tell she was hesitant because she paused.

"Come on," she answered, and I reversed my truck and parked in the spot a couple of cars away from her.

We end up walking into the doctor's office, and I sat down while she checked in. I could tell she was trying to be hard, but I knew I would break her down, eventually. She waddled her ass over to me and sat down next to me. She tried to pretend to be occupied in her phone.

"You know I miss you, right, Lace?" I asked. Lace paused, and then she turned to me.

"Look, Del, this isn't going to be like old times. Juan and I are back together. So whatever you have in mind, forget about it," she whispered.

The nurse called Lace's name before I could even respond. As I followed her back to the room, my phone started ringing. Looking at the screen, I had pressed ignore. A text came through

Boss: *Drop in twenty, get there!*

Shaking my head, I knew I had to leave. Standing up, I walked over to Lace.

"Look, it's an emergency, and I got to head out, but can you please call me and let me know how everything goes?" I asked.

Lace nodded her head, and I leaned down and placed a kiss on her forehead. It probably was wrong to do, but I couldn't resist.

Chapter Twenty-Seven

JUAN

Since Lace left this morning, I couldn't help but think about this shit with Lovey. I ain't no deadbeat ass nigga, so why in the hell would she wait all this time to tell me some shit like that? She knows where I be, and she most definitely know my number, so for her to randomly call, this ain't sitting right. I can't lose Lace again, hell no.

Pulling into City Gear, I started to back in a parking spot when this other car came flying in, causing me to stop.

"The fuck?" I snapped.

They continued to park they car, and I backed on in. The nigga that hopped out was so busy talking on the phone that he wasn't even paying attention. When I saw that curly ass ponytail, I knew who it was. That nigga Del wasn't even paying attention to his surroundings. I got on out the car and walked in the store. My eyes landed on him at the wall asking someone for a shoe size. I stayed behind but could hear his conversation.

"Yeah, I ran into shorty at the Mapco today. She was big as hell. She said she was about seven months."

I inched a little closer because I knew he was talking about Lace.

"I asked her was the baby mine. She says maybe then gone try to pull off. I followed that ass, and we ended up at the doctor's office and talked for a bit. Check this though she said that nigga Juan supposed to have a baby by Lovey. Yeah, Lo's baby mama. I don't know what that nigga got going on, but he needs to keep that shit up so I can get my girl back." He laughed.

The girl came from the back carrying his shoes. Del turned around to walk to the counter, and we looked dead at each other. This nigga hit me with a head nod. I was mugging the shit out of him, and we were about to get to the bottom of this.

"So, you ran into Lace today?" I asked. He said something in the phone then placed it in his pocket.

"I sure did run into her. We talked about her seed she's carrying since it's a possibility the little nigga's mine." He laughed and walked off towards the register.

"Nigga, I wasn't done talking to you."

"Look, homie. Don't be walking up on me like you know me. I don't know what the fuck Lace told you or who you think I am, but I ain't the one. It ain't nothing else to rap about. You did you, she did her, and now there's a baby in question. That's between you and Lace though, or shall I say you and Lovey," Del said as he grabbed his bags and headed out the door.

I couldn't believe this nigga just played me like that.

———

When I walked into the house, Lace was in the kitchen, eating a turkey sandwich and glued to her Kindle. She looked up at me and then rolled her eyes. I don't know why the fuck she was still mad at me because she had some explaining to do.

"I'm gone tell you this shit now. You better get that bitch Lovey in check because she fucking inboxed me today on Facebook talking about since you ain't answering your phone, she's contacting me. I'm not about to deal with your baby mama drama!" she spat.

If looks could kill, Lace's ass would be dead right about now.

"Since you throwing orders around when were you gone tell me you ran into your other baby daddy today?" I asked, crossing my arms. Lace shook her head.

"Honestly, when I saw you. It wasn't shit to me, so why would I hide it? He saw me at Mapco. We talked for a minute then I drove off, and he followed me to the doctor. I told him I would call him when the baby was born to do a DNA test. Then he asked me how you felt about it, and I told you were straight, and I happened to mention the Lovey situation. Del then told me that Lovey was messing around with Lo. You should check into that." Lace shrugged all nonchalant.

"That shit was none of his fucking business, Lace. Plus, Lovey might be my baby mama, so I don't see a problem with her hitting you up if she can't get in touch with me." I shrugged as well, being petty with my last statement. Lace hopped up off the stool.

"That's what the fuck your cell phone is for. That bitch doesn't need to be all in my inbox. Since she supposed to be your baby mama, you need to answer your phone. You want to trip about me running into Del as if I want that nigga. You just remember you came back to me. I was good by myself, and I'm not about to go through all this shit every time you decide you want to mention Del name. I'm not finna put up with Lovey's shit either. So you need to make up your mind about what it is you want?"

"You know what. I need time to think," I threw out there, regretting that shit as soon as it slipped out my mouth.

"I'm not no merry-go-round, Juan. You may miss your turn the next time," Lace said a bit too calm for me. Her phone started ringing.

"This is the shit I'm talking about. Now the hoe is calling me from Messenger. Bitch, why is you calling me on here?" Lace yelled in the phone.

"Where is Juan?" Lovey asked.

"Bitch you about to get blocked now. That nigga got a phone. Call that raggedy motherfucker!" Lace yelled, hanging up the phone. I watched as she closed her eyes and counted to ten. Looking back at me, she pointed towards the door.

"You're dismissed," was all she said, and I did just that. When I left out, my ass was about to bump down on Lovey because she was doing way too much.

Chapter Twenty-Eight

BRIELLE

Standing outside of the airport, I was waiting for Lace to pull up. My trip to the Bahamas was much needed. I needed a break for myself taking a vacation from this shit show called life. Lace pulled up and popped the trunk. Rolling my suitcase to the back of the car, I placed my bags in the trunk and got in the front seat.

"Sup bitch, you miss me? You could've helped me with my bags," I joked.

"Girl, I ain't lifting shit with this belly. Stop playing with me," she answered and pulled out.

"I'm so glad to be back. It was fun and all, but I slick got homesick. How's shit been going with you?" I asked.

The way Lace sighed, I leaned to the side and adjusted my seatbelt because I knew it was some tea.

"Girl, what the fuck didn't happen. Let me tell your ass why this nigga done up and left again..."

Lace started to tell me everything that had transpired, and this was the reason why I was team Del. Juan was a jealous ass nigga, and it was showing all the while his dirt was catching up with him. I knew Del had moved back, and I'm so glad he finally ran into Lace.

"Lace, you need to let that nigga be. I know you trying to do right by your child, but that nigga is bogus. Who the fuck wants to deal with all that shit, and if that's his baby mama, you gone have to drag that hoe one good time. Otherwise, she finna keep being messy," I admitted.

I could tell Lace was thinking about what I had said. Lace's phone started to ring, and she answered on Bluetooth.

"Yeah, wassup?" she spoke.

"Is that how you answer the phone, shorty?" a voice who wasn't Juan came through the speakers. A smile etched my face, and I looked at Lace, who was blushing.

"Delmazio, what's up my long lost brother!" I screamed.

"Who is that, Brielle? Wassup, girl?"

"What do you want, Del?" Lace asked. She could pretend all she wanted to, but she missed that nigga.

"I was seeing if you ate. I was going to bring you something to eat."

"I'm not even at home," she started to say, and I interrupted her.

"She's dropping me off, and then she will be home. Fuck that. You know her pregnant ass always hungry." I laughed.

"Brielle!" she shrieked.

"Bet, shoot me your address and what you want?" was all Del said before hanging up before Lace could reject.

"You get on my nerves," Lace whined.

"Fuck that. If that nigga Juan wants to play and leave to get his head together as he says, you can get your head together and belly full with the man you supposed to be with anyway. Things happen for a reason. Ain't it weird how he just called you, and at the perfect time," I smirked.

Chapter Twenty-Nine

LACE

When I pulled up at Brielle's house, I couldn't wait for her ass to get out. After thinking about what she said, it made sense. Del calling right now was the perfect timing, and I was going to take advantage of it. If Juan wanted to act an ass, then he got it.

As soon as I got home, I took a quick shower and straightened up the living room a little. I had a lot of nervous energy because what if this nigga popped up while Del was here. A text came to my phone, and it was Del letting me know that he was pulling up. Making my way to the door, I watched as he pulled in and got out carrying our food.

As he neared the door, I moved to the side to let him in the house. By the smell of his cologne and the familiar scent of his hair, I could tell he used the same stuff he did when we were younger. These pregnancy hormones had my senses on ten.

"The kitchen is right through there," I told Del and pointed down the hall. Locking up, I made sure to put the latch on the door just in case Juan wanted to bring his ass back through here tonight.

Walking into the kitchen, I watched as Del placed the food on the counter and started to move around the kitchen as if he knew what he was doing.

"What made you call and ask me about some food that was so random?" I asked him. Del stopped what he was doing, and his facial expression changed.

"Well, I had planned on calling you earlier, but I got side-tracked, then I went over to my homie's house." He paused and shook his head.

"What are you shaking your head for?" I quizzed.

"My homeboy just so happens to be associated with someone that knows Juan. Juan was there, and he was hugged up on Lovey. It was as if he didn't care that he was seen either. That nigga and I had a run-in earlier too. He called himself trying to check me, but that shit ain't fly. He out here being real reckless. He can have that, though. I'm trying to be the one you need."

"I put that nigga out, so yeah, he probably was with that hoe. Don't she mess with this nigga Lo that I keep hearing everybody talk about?" I asked.

Del slid me my food, and I climbed up on the stool.

"Real shit, from what I know, he fucks with her tough because that's his baby mama."

"How many damn kids she got?"

"That hoe got one kid, a son," Del said.

Lovey's out here trying to put the next nigga kid on Juan and for what? I hate hoes like that, and then he's all over in that bitch's face.

"Look, though. I didn't come over here to spend the whole time talking about that nigga. What's on your mental right now? Considering this baby situation, do you see your-self being with Juan when it obvious that he's not man enough to stop playing games?" Del asked me.

I became silent and let his words play repeatedly. It was

safe to say that I wanted them both. Of course, I missed the relationship Del and I had, but we were young, and our little fling was just that when we got grown. I was with Juan eight whole years, and shit was just up and down now. Rubbing my temples, I let out a deep sigh and shrugged my shoulders.

"Del, I don't know. Truthfully, at times, I want Juan to be the dad, and then sometimes I want it to be you. My head is so messed up right now. This is just a lot. I just need to focus on delivering my baby and making sure he is healthy."

Del finished his food, and then both of us cleaned up our mess and headed to the living room. I sat down on the couch, and he sat on the other placing my feet in his lap. We continued to share our thoughts and old memories while he massaged my feet. I could get used to this if I allowed it. The only thing I needed and wanted was peace.

Chapter Thirty

LACE

Baby's Here

"I really don't feel like walking around this damn mall," I complained to Brielle.

I was a week overdue, and she got the bright idea to walk laps around Opry Mills. My son was being stubborn, and I wondered where he got that shit from, but he wasn't budging and wanting to come out just yet. I waddled my ass into Footlocker and headed to the women's side, looking for me some tennis shoes.

"Lace, ain't that Lovey over there with her son?" Brielle tapped me on my shoulder. She signaled in the direction she was looking, and my eyes followed.

"Yep, that sho is that bitch. I never saw her son, but if that's him, he doesn't look like no damn Juan. Who is that nigga with her?" I asked. This nigga must be the dude Lo everyone linked her with. Look at them, looking like a happy family.

"He looks like the pappy is who he looks like," Brielle joked, and we both started laughing.

"Oh, well, she's lucky I'm about to pop and don't need to

be fighting," I told Brielle. After getting the stuff I needed, I headed to the register and took my place in line.

"Lace, is that you?" I turned around to see Lovey standing there with her items.

"You must be putting on in front of your nigga. You don't know me like that!" I spat and turned back around.

This hoe was picking, and I knew that shit. Giving the cashier the cash, I grabbed my bags and turned around to walk out. Lovey had a permanent mug on her face.

"I got you so bothered." I laughed and met up with Brielle and walked out of the store. A wave of exhaustion swept over me.

"Aye, I think I'm done. I done got sleepy," I yawned. Brielle rolled her eyes.

"Girl, come on. You done got in your feelings and shit," she had the nerve to say.

"Brielle, this ain't the time to play because I know that's what you're doing. I don't have any reason to be in my feelings. That hoe in there with a whole different man that doesn't belong to me." I sighed as we walked out the mall.

As soon as we got in the car, I laid my seat back and closed my eyes, and then thats when the sharpest pain shot across my stomach.

"Ouch!" I yelled.

"You okay?" Brielle asked.

I nodded my head as I rubbed my stomach, and then another pain came after that. When I felt the seat of my pants getting warm, I knew it was something, or I had just pissed on myself.

"Brielle, either I just pissed in your seat, or my water just broke. The way these pains are coming, you need to take me straight to the hospital!" I yelled.

Brielle put her foot on the gas and floored it to the hospital. The contractions were coming back to back, so I grabbed my phone and called Juan. I don't know why he was the first person I decided to call. This nigga didn't even answer the phone, so I called Del.

"Wassup?" he answered.

"I'm on the way to the hospital right now. It's time!" I called out in between breaths.

"On the way," he said and ended the call.

Brielle whipped into the emergency entrance in ten minutes. Del was waiting there with a wheelchair. Just seeing him was a relief. I had tried Juan and left a message, but I guess he didn't care.

"I'm going to go to your house and get your bag, then I'll be right back!" Brielle told me. Nodding my head, I laid back in the chair as Del pushed me to Labor and Delivery.

When we got out of the elevator, the nurses immediately knew what it was the way I was breathing. They got me settled in a room, and things from there happened fast. The contractions were getting closer and closer. Damn, could I have the damn epidural or something?

Del sat off to the side and tried to feed me some damn ice chips. Brielle came back in there, and we locked eyes. She shook her head no because she had tried to get in touch with Juan and still no answer. Fuck him.

Del was unusually quiet the entire time. I wanted to speak on it, but I was in too much pain until he noticed I looked at him. Del stood up and made his way closer to me.

"Lace, I asked the doctor to perform a test soon as the baby gets here. She said ok. I decided if the baby isn't mine I would leave you alone and let you be with Juan. I hate to lose you again, but I don't want to come in between the two of you and your son." He sighed.

I closed my eyes and turned my head because I felt this was goodbye, and I didn't like this feeling.

———

The wailing sounds of my son could be heard across the room as they wiped him clean. Brielle was crying tears of joy as if she had pushed him out her damn self. The moment they brought him to me and I laid eyes on him, I knew I would never love another the way I loved him this quickly. This was mine and belonged to me. I couldn't believe I created something so precious.

My son weighed seven pounds, eleven ounces. Looking at him, I couldn't tell if he looked like Juan or Del because they both were the same complexion, and he was white as hell. He had my eyes and jet-black curly hair. Welcome to my chaotic world, son.

Chapter Thirty-One

DELMAZIO

To hit Lace with that news about her son, I didn't want to do it while she was in labor, but I didn't want to start to get attached to this baby, and he wasn't mine. I had to protect my heart. There was no way I wanted to leave her, but if the test came back, and he wasn't mine, I just felt like a part of her wanted to make things work with Juan.

The last few weeks between us had been amazing since Juan's been gone, but I can tell I didn't have Lace fully. She made a mistake getting with Juan. Lace's heart wasn't fully in it and now look at this shit.

Watching Lace give birth was an experience I'm glad I got to see because it made me love her more. Looking at him, I felt he wasn't mine. I felt disconnected, but I could be wrong. He did look a little foreign, though, but I guess we would have to wait for the results to come back. When the nurse gave Lace him to hold, she broke down. Seeing her in mother form melted my heart.

"You want to hold him?" she asked. My hands were shoved down in my pockets, and I just stood there.

"Nall, I'd rather not, I think I should head out," I admitted. Lace screwed up her face.

"Del, I understand that you might be having mixed emotions about this, but this standoffish act isn't you. You holding him isn't going to change anything. Why are you being this way?" she started to cry. My shoulders slumped in defeat, and I walked near the bed.

"Stop crying before you upset him. Lace, I want to love you and not from a distance. I want you to be mine and only mine like we used to be in high school. I gave up so much because I loved you, and shit ain't changed. I don't want to get attached to him, and he isn't mine. Who's to say that Juan still holds a piece of your heart, and as soon as he pops up, it's you and him back against the world?" I admitted.

"Juan hasn't been around, and he missed all of this. I have never stopped loving you, even when I was with him. How could I ever forget the things you have done for me and the way you gave up your life to protect me? I wanted to ride it out with you, but when you told me you were going to Memphis, the same day I got that letter, Juan popped up. Yes, I love him, but I'm not in love with him anymore. I love what we had before the infidelity on both our parts, and his continued cheating is what pushed me away. He left me to go be with the one person that started all this shit years ago. My son means everything to me, and I want to be happy and raise him. My question to you is, what if I want to be with you, and he's not yours?" she asked.

I climbed in the bed beside her and looked down at him sleeping peacefully.

"That is a good question, ain't it?" I laughed and reached for him. Lace handed him over, and soon as he got in my arms my heart swoll.

"What you gone do about, Juan?" I asked.

"Del, what is there to do? Honestly, Juan has been doing

him since he left my damn house to go be with Lovey. I told him that shit was going to get old. I've called him since I went in labor, and he has yet to return my call. Fuck him. Landon Kole. That's it, that's what I want to name him," she blurted out.

Looking down at the baby, he looked like a Landon.

"Landon it is, and it even fits if he turns out to have the last name Davis," I joked.

We both started laughing, and the door flew open. We both looked at the door, and Juan stood there. All I did was shake my head at this nigga.

"Damn, a nigga don't answer the phone, and you got the next nigga up here playing daddy?" Juan looked at Lace.

"First of all, don't come in here talking reckless. I'm so sick of your tired ass. I called both of you, but you know what I called you several times before I called him, I even called you up until I had him. Don't come in here with all that bull-shit when you've been missing in action, living your life. Del has already taken a blood test, so I will contact you once his results come in. I have nothing else to say to you!" Lace spat.

"Can I at least see him?" he had the nerve to ask her. I handed the baby to Lace and stood up.

"I'm gone run down to the cafeteria and give you two some time to talk," I said, leaning in to kiss Lace on the forehead.

Walking past Juan, I shook my head and laughed at that nigga as I walked by because I knew whatever he tried to say Lace was mine now and wasn't going anywhere.

Chapter Thirty-Two

JUAN

My ass was on a run in Murfreesboro when Lace called, and then a nigga started freaking out. I was trying my best to get down here as fast as I could. What I wasn't expecting was walking in here and seeing her all in Del's face looking like one big happy family.

A nigga's been going through it since I left the house. Yeah, I fucked up and fell back in Lovey's trap, but she was just playing a nigga big time. She already knew who the fuck her baby daddy was, and just like everyone was saying, it was Lo. They had broken up, and she was talking that reckless shit to him talking about he wasn't the daddy.

Del left out the room, and I walked closer to the bed, and Lace turned the baby around where I could see him. I was hoping to at least see some type of resemblance, but it was nothing. Was I wrong because I didn't want to hold him?

"So, are you and Del back together?" I asked.

"What are you doing here, Juan? You come to see the baby, or are you worried about my personal life?" she replied.

Damn.

"I got your messages, and I wasn't in the city, but once I

took care of business, I came straight here. A nigga was
scared. I had to get up the courage to come see you. I owe
you an apology for leaving the way I did. Come to find out
Lovey's son wasn't mine. She was on some get-back shit with
her nigga. I was hoping to come here and get you and my son
back."

Lace busted out laughing, and that shit pissed me off.

"Juan, oh so you want to come back since things didn't
work out with the Lovey situation. You should've known that
hoe was playing you in the first place. However, you put me
to the side and chased after that and left me hanging as if I
wasn't shit. You don't get to pick and choose when you fuck
with me. As I said, I'm tired of your shit. Who the fuck
wants to keep going back and forth. This shit is getting old."
She sighed. The baby started to shift in her arms, and she
placed her focus on him.

"What's his name?" I decided to ask.

"Landon Kole," she mumbled and went back to tending
to him.

"Lace, I really love you, and I hope that you can see a
nigga forreal."

"Juan, I love you too, but not like you want me to
anymore. If Landon is your child, I will not stand in the way
of you being in his life, but other than that, what we had is
gone. I'm sorry," she said somberly.

Biting my lip, I nodded my head and headed towards the
door. The door flew open, and it was Lace's dad.

"Juan," was all he said and flew over to the bed. I felt all
that animosity.

"Aite, just call and let me know the deal," I told her and
left out the room.

Damn, I was expecting to get my girl back. I'm sure she
done told her daddy all kinds of bullshit because that nigga
used to rock with me, but he couldn't even look at me. Once

the elevator stopped, I walked out of the hospital and headed across the street.

Getting in the car, I sat there and laid my head on the seat.

"So was the baby yours?"

"It's too early to tell, but she had Del do a blood test, so we just gone wait for the results."

"You need to get a test for yourself as well because hell, what if she's sleeping with somebody else?"

"On some real shit, can you just shut up and pull off? You so worried about me, but hell, your so-called nigga was in there with her looking like a big ass family," I told Bianca.

I met Bianca a few weeks back, and we kicked it off. She looked familiar when I saw her, and she approached me, saying the same thing. She attended my wedding with Del. She and Del had a small fling. She claimed it was nothing serious. Yeah, I know I wasn't shit for trying to get Lace back, and the whole time was still on some fuck shit, but I couldn't help who I loved.

EPILOGUE

Lace

Trying to get settled after the blow that hit me was actually smooth. When the results finally came back from the DNA test for Landon, my heart was crushed when it revealed Landon belonged to Juan. The shit was beyond devastating. Del remained the man he was, and even though I knew the news hurt him, he continued as if nothing had changed, Landon was now three months old. In the weirdest way, Landon looked like Del, and I couldn't understand why.

At this point in my life, I thought it would be hard dealing with Juan, but he delivered another shocking blow. A week after I had Landon, he was arrested on a drug trafficking charge. When he was arrested, some girl name Bianca reached out to me and told me who she was, and I was to direct any messages for him to her. When the results came back that Landon was his, this nigga had the nerve to say he wanted to sign his rights over. Juan was a pure bitch, and I just can't see why I never saw that shit.

My life moved forward because I could and would not dwell on a toxic part of my life. I deserved to be happy and finally at peace. Everything that I ever encountered made me stronger when I shouldn't even be standing. Del came in my life, and he secured my heart and protected it. The darkest part of my life had me sheltered and hiding, then there Del was waiting to unravel me piece-by-piece. Life continued even though it was to the beat of a chaotic song.

Standing in the doorway, I watched as Del and Landon slept peacefully. I had a client this morning, but I couldn't sleep anyway, so I was up before time. I removed my AirPods from my ear and eased over to the bed. Del shifted in his sleep.

"You know a nigga ain't fully asleep and you over here watching me and shit," he whispered.

"I'm just enjoying this peace while I can. Y'all looked cute." I laughed.

Del slowly slid Landon off his arm and placed him beside him. He sat up on the side of the bed, shirtless with sweatpants on. His long hair wasn't in its usual ponytail, so it laid flawlessly over his shoulders. Gazing at him, I felt myself getting all misty-eyed.

"Lace, you're creeping me out. Why you over there in your head?" he asked.

"I can't help it. You're fine as hell, and I was just admiring how blessed I was to have you."

"Is that right?" He chuckled.

Del stood up and headed to the bathroom to take care of his morning breath. Shaking my head, I started to get dressed for work and my cell started to ring. Looking at the screen, I didn't recognize the number.

"Hello," I answered.

"Yes, is this a Ms. Tucker?" the person on the end asked.

"Yes, what is this in regards to?" I snapped. I hated for a motherfucker to call my phone on some bullshit.

"This is the warden at the Tennessee Correction Facility, and you were listed as next to kin for a Juan Price. I'm sorry to inform you, but there was a situation that took place, and Mr. Price was pronounced dead a few moments ago," she said.

My mouth widened, and I looked at the phone in shock. Del came back in the room and stopped in his tracks.

"Um ok, I'm not sure why I was still listed, but I can try to get in touch with someone for you. Thank you for calling," I panicked and hung up the phone. Looking at Del, he lifted his brow.

"What's going on?" he asked.

"That was the warden where Juan is locked up, and she said that Juan was dead." I sighed, and a few tears actually dropped. Juan was an ass, but at one point, it wasn't all bad. I didn't wish death on him like I did NaQuan.

"It's going to be okay. Damn, did they say what happened?" I shook my head no.

"Just that a situation occurred, and they pronounced him dead," I sighed, and I looked at a sleeping Landon. Del wrapped his arms around me.

"Landon will be okay too." He rubbed his hands over my head, adjusting a few strands I had flying.

"Please don't ever leave me," I begged.

"Girl, you finally done unraveled that tangled mess your life was in and have blossomed to a beautiful queen. You think I would leave you? I love you, Lace, and our future is so bright." Del leaned in and placed his lips on mine.

When we kissed, I felt my soul lift to his, and I knew everything was going to be all alright for my son and me. Maybe we would have our own children someday and get married. The world was open for us, and all the endless possibilities welcomed me.

The End

KYEATE'S CATALOG

Thank you for reading please leave a review and make sure you check out my catalog below.

Games He Play: Di'mond & Kyng
A Savage and his Lady (Series 1& 2)
Masking My Pain
Fiyah & Desire: Down to ride for a Boss
Securing the Bag and His Heart (Series)
Securing the Bag and His Heart Too
Remnants (Novella)
5 Miles Until Empty (Novella)
Once Upon a Hood Love: A Nashville Fairytale (Novella)
Tricked: A Halloween Love Story (Novella)
Kali Kusain: Counterfeit Queen
Dear Saint Nik: A Christmas Novella
My First Night with You: A BWWM Novella
Enticed by a Cold-Hearted Menace
Me vs. Me: Life of Deceit

Her Mended Soul
Taking a Thug's Love
Valuable Pain: Money, Lies, & Heartbreak
Eboneigh: A Boss Christmas Tale
Unsteady Love From A Thug

ME VS. ME: LIFE OF DECEIT

Her Mended Soul

Taking a Thug's Love
Valuable Pain: Money, Lies, & Heartbreak
Eboneigh: A Boss Christmas Tale
Unsteady Love From A Thug

AVAILABLE NOW ON AMAZON KINDLE

Unsteady Love From A Thug
Eze (Easy) Sadiq

"Yes, Eze!" ole girl called out as I hit her with full force long deep strokes. With each thrust, she was throwing that ass back. Sweat dripped from my chest, falling onto her back. It was hot as a bitch in here, and I was trying like hell not to succumb to my death while trying to catch a nut.

"Fuck me, baby!" she screamed.

I ain't have time for all this theatric shit, and I wasn't a talker during sex. All I needed was something warm to catch this nut, and then I'm gone. Using my free hand, I reached forward and grabbed her hair, wrapping my hand in her hair.

"Damn Eze, don't pull too hard. This is a wig," she complained.

Irritated off that shit alone, I used my hand and shoved her head forward, pressing that shit into the mattress. With both hands on her hips, I closed my eyes and continued stroking. I had to get this shit up out of me and fast. Time was cutting it close. My phone dinged, which was on the nightstand, so I looked down at my watch, and the text I was waiting on came through.

"Catch this shit," I demanded while pulling my dick out.

While she turned around towards me, I snatched the condom off. She was ready too, tongue all out, holding her breast. All I could do was smirk at the thought that popped in my head. In one quick motion, I yanked her wig off her head and nutted on her Cleo's.

"What the fuck, Eze?" she yelled, and I placed the wig back on top of her head.

"I was just making sure your wig was secured," I laughed and took off towards the bathroom. I know I wasn't shit, and nobody needed to tell me what I already knew.

As soon as I got in the bathroom, I looked around in the closet for a clean rag. Grabbing some soap, I cleaned my dick off getting it back fresh. Looking in the mirror, I grinned and ran my tongue across my gold teeth. With no time to waste, I headed back out to the bedroom to get my shit because I had to bounce. She was so pissed at my ass that she ain't even look my way.

"Aite, then I holla at ya," I said before exiting the room.

"Eze, you not gone give me no money for my hair? That shit was trifling." She pouted.

"That shit will wash out, girl. You done caught my nut in far worse places. I got to go. I got you next time." I hit her with the deuce and headed out.

When stepping outside, I pulled my hoodie over my head and hit the remote start on my truck. It was cold as hell out here, and I left my coat in the truck. I didn't have time taking all my shit in gal's house. As soon as I got in the truck, I placed my hands together and blew into them. After a few minutes, I pulled my phone out to get the address off the text that had come to my phone. It was time to go to work.

Most people would look down on my job description, but

it had me eating well. At twenty-five, I wasn't your average street nigga. Hell, I probably was worse depending on how you look at it. I wasn't into selling drugs. I used my gift of hands differently. Pulling off, I headed to the secret location of today's job.

Life for me consisted of one thing, and that was money. Money was the only thing I could possess that I controlled. It didn't hurt me, and it didn't betray me like the average human. Now money can make people do those things, but I didn't have that problem because nobody got close enough to harm me in that way. It was only me out here. A nigga wasn't in a relationship, had no children, and no family. I had one nigga that was my right hand, and that was it.

Pulling up at the location, I cut the engine and peeped the scene. The lot was full, so I knew it was about to be a big money night. That shit made my dick hard thinking of the cash out at the end of the night. Reaching into the glove box, I pulled out my brush and went over my waves a few times. Tossing it back in the box, I got out and headed to the money.

Walking into the building, it was already live, and shit ain't even started yet. Scanning the place, I was just peeping the scene and the faces. Mostly everyone there was regulars.

"Bossman!" I heard, and I turned around. It was my right-hand man, Bullet.

"How we looking?" I flat out asked.

"Shit's looking good. The new girls Diego sent are all lined up in the back," he answered. I nodded my head and followed him.

We walked through the crowd and into a sealed-off room. Entering the room, all the chatter stopped, and all eyes were on me.

"Y'all line up and face him!" Bullet demanded. It was four

girls, and they all did as they were told with frightened looks on their faces.

"Diego said these three are worth every penny you paid for. Now this one, Diego said he threw her in because she just had to go, and he hopes like hell you could do something with her." Bullet laughed his ugly ass laugh.

I glanced up at the girl that he was talking about, and she looked innocent and out of place. Directing my focus back on all of them, I crossed my arms and rubbed my facial hairs.

"Who in here knows how to fight?" I asked. They all looked at each other crazy, but nobody said anything.

"That was a motherfucking question!" I yelled.

My eyes landed on a thick, chocolate chick. She had attitude all over her. Walking up to her face, she gave me that look that most chicks gave me when they wanted dick dropped off in them.

"Can you fight?"

"I-I mean I can do a little something," she stuttered.

"You up first, but let me tell you something. This fight is one for your freedom. You can either make me some money or cause me to lose some money. I suggest you make me some because if you lose my money. You'll work that shit off until I get it back. Diego ain't sent you over here for nothing!" I spat and stepped back.

"As for the rest of you, I suggest you sit back and watch because you all gone get in the ring before the night over with. Bullet, take them to the box so they can watch and you 'Ms. I can do a little something' bring your ass!" I snapped and made my way back out to the front, where the crowd was ready for the first match.

Growing up, I stayed fighting. I could break every bone in a nigga's face with my bare hands. I had to find a way to direct my pain, and fighting was my passion, so I turned that shit into a profit by starting an underground female fight club. That was the best shit I ever did. It was hard to find females to fight, so I would cop them from this Mexican cat, Diego. Diego was into some other shit. I knew he was into trafficking girls, so for a price, he would send me special ones.

A lot of girls that came through here, I would let go, and a lot once they saw the amount of money they were bringing in would leave but remained fighters for me. I was all about the money, so I didn't care what lives they had before me or after. Hell, all I kept up with was the names and the amount of money they were making me. To make things better, I trained majority of the females to be some lethal heavy hitters.

My fight club was special invite-only, and every fight night I would have damn near two hundred spectators. Thursdays-Saturdays were fight nights, and nobody knew the location until an hour beforehand.

My folks paid a hundred dollars a pop to see a fight, so you do the math on how much I was bringing in a night. That doesn't even include bets and wagers on the girls.

Making my way up to the ring, I held the rope so that gal could get in. If she wasn't scared before, she looked that way now.

"Aite motherfuckers, put your money where your mouth is, we got a newcomer tonight!" I roared, and everybody started yelling and barking. The adrenaline that gave me was everything. It was fight night and money to be made.

CPSIA information can be obtained
at www.ICGtesting.com
Printed in the USA
LVHW111623260220
648289LV00003B/532

9 798605 296485